HAUNTING CHRISTMAS TALES

Scholastic Children's Books
Scholastic Publications Ltd,
7–9 Pratt Street, London NW1 0AE, UK

Scholastic Inc,
730 Broadway, New York, NY 10003, USA

Scholastic Canada Ltd,
123 Newkirk Road, Richmond Hill,
Ontario, Canada L4C 3G5

Ashton Scholastic Pty Ltd,
P O Box 579, Gosford, New South Wales,
Australia

Ashton Scholastic Ltd,
Private Bag 1, Penrose, Auckland,
New Zealand

First published by Scholastic Publications Ltd, 1991

This collection copyright © Scholastic Publications Ltd, 1991
Illustrations copyright © David Wyatt, 1991

ISBN 0590 76615 5

Made and printed by Richard Clay, Bungay, Suffolk

HAUNTING CHRISTMAS TALES

Ghost stories for the festive season

Includes stories by
Joan Aiken · Garry Kilworth · Robert Swindells

Scholastic Hardcover
Scholastic Publications Limited
London

ACKNOWLEDGEMENTS

All of the stories are original and appear for the first time in this volume. 300427011

The following are the copyright owners of the stories:

Crespian and Clairan © Joan Aiken, 1991
The Investigators © David Belbin, 1991
The Other Room © Jill Bennett, 1991
The Woodman's Enigma © Garry Kilworth, 1991
Jingle Bells © Tessa Krailing, 1991
The Cracked Smile © Anthony Masters, 1991
Across the Fields © Susan Price, 1991
The Chime Child © Ian Strachan, 1991
The Weeping Maid © Robert Swindells, 1991

The publisher wishes to thank all of the above, and David Wyatt, the illustrator, for their work and enthusiasm for this collection.

ontents   Page

JINGLE BELLS

Tessa Krailing

hree days to Christmas and I was looking forward to it. Imagine, me looking forward to Christmas! Usually I dreaded it.

But this year, for the first time since I could remember, there would be no haunting. We had left the ghost behind when we moved house a month ago. Now, at last, we were free of it.

Or so I thought.

"Nine-thirty," Mum said. "Time you were in bed, Anna love."

I got to my feet without arguing. Since we had moved into our new house I no longer minded going upstairs after dark, not even three nights before Christmas. I patted my father's bald spot in passing. "'Night, Dad."

He grunted, not taking his eyes off the TV screen. Dad was a man of few words. I couldn't recall ever hearing him string a whole sentence together.

When I reached the door Mum said, "Look in on Becky, will you, love? Just check she's all right."

"Okay."

I ran upstairs to find my four-year-old sister fast asleep, her straight fair hair fanned out over the pillow. As I bent to remove the teddy bear slipping from her grasp I glanced at her face and paused. Was it my imagination or did she look a little flushed? And her breathing . . . it seemed very shallow. Perhaps the quilt was too high. I pulled it down, away from her face, and at that moment she stirred and opened her eyes.

When she saw me she smiled. "I just heard him," she said.

"Heard who?"

"Santa. He went past my window."

An unpleasant suspicion gripped me. "How did you know it was Santa?"

She looked at me as if I were being exceptionally stupid. "I heard the bells, of course. The jingle bells on his sleigh."

I shivered, then straightened up. "That's impossible. It's too early for Santa. He won't come till Christmas Eve."

She frowned, puzzled. "Who was it, then?"

"How should I know?"

I had spoken too sharply. She looked hurt. In a softer voice I said, "I expect you were dreaming. Don't worry, Santa will bring you lots of presents when the time comes. 'Night, Becky." I dropped a kiss on her forehead and automatically reached over to switch off the lamp, then remembered it had to be left on. Dad hadn't got around to fixing up a night-light yet.

8

Outside on the landing I paused, trying to take in what Becky had said. The sound of bells . . . outside her window . . . three days before Christmas. So we hadn't left the ghost behind in our old house, as I had hoped. No, it had come with us.

I lay in my bed that night, waiting for the haunting to start. The bells were only the beginning: the rest was a nightmare. For years I had suffered it, Christmas after Christmas, keeping silent because I knew my parents wouldn't believe me. They were both far too down-to-earth. Dad was a farmer, interested only in fatstock prices and the quality of sileage, while Mum kept busy with her poultry.

But a month ago Dad was forced to give up farming because of back trouble. That's why we'd had to leave the two hundred-year-old farmhouse we had lived in all our lives and move into town so that Mum could go back to nursing, which is what she used to do before she married Dad. Our new home was white-fronted and semi-detached, built about twenty-five years ago, on a typical surburban housing estate. Not at all the sort of place you'd expect to be haunted.

A door closed. That was Mum going into the bedroom. Dad had gone shortly before, so now they were both in bed and the house was quiet. I switched on my bedside lamp. Not that having the light on made any difference, but it was preferable to lying in the dark.

Maybe Becky had imagined it. She'd never mentioned

hearing the bells before. But then she'd only been three last Christmas. At three years old, if you hear bells outside your window, you don't think to query it.

The church clock struck midnight and my eyelids were beginning to droop. Then, very faintly, I heard them. Bells. Jingling. Becky was right – it did sound like a reindeer's harness. Gentle, harmless little chimes. I lay there, listening, my heart thumping with fear.

Next came the tapping at the window. I stiffened, tense as a board. Tap, tap. Tap, tap. The wretched thing, whatever it was wanted to come in. It always wanted to come in. Luckily I had taken the precaution of shutting the ventilator before I got into bed. I'd rather suffocate than let it inside.

That was the next stage, of course. Suffocation.

I fought it off as long as I could. Ghosts, I knew, were supposed to be heralded by a drop in temperature, an icy coldness in the atmosphere. But this one was different. It brought heat – a sweltering, airless, oppressive heat. I wrenched open the neck of my nightdress – my long-sleeved winter nightdress, which buttoned right up to the chin. Usually I was glad of its cosiness, but not tonight. I threw back the bedclothes, gasping for breath. The heat was all around me, like a thick heavy blanket, stifling and choking . . .

I swung my legs out of bed and staggered over to the window. Now I was far more frightened of what was inside the room than of what might be lurking outside. Coughing and retching, I struggled with the latch, certain I had only seconds left to live.

At last I succeeded. I hung over the ledge, taking in great gulps of cold night air. Filling my lungs with it, breathing deeply . . . until at last the panic began to subside and I collapsed against the window-sill, all the fight gone out of me, not able to move.

Then came the final touch, the same as always. The bells again, faintly jingling, fading into the distance. Gone. For tonight, at any rate. Tomorrow would be a different story.

After a while I closed the window, switched off the lamp and crawled back into bed. I was exhausted, drained of all energy. At some point – I've no idea when – I must have slipped from waking into sleep, because when I next opened my eyes it was to the grey light of dawn.

"Your sister comes today," Mum reminded Dad at breakfast. "She should be arriving about tea-time."

Becky gave a shriek of delight. "I *love* Auntie Jen! Do you think she'll like our new house?"

"I hope so," Mum said dryly. "She would never spend Christmas with us at the farmhouse because she said it was cold. Mind you, she'll find that box room a bit on the pokey side."

"She can have my room," I said. "I don't mind moving out." Stupid, I know; but I had this sudden hope that if I slept somewhere different the ghost might not be able to find me.

"Well, if you're sure . . ." Mum peered into my face. "Anna, are you feeling all right? You look rather pale."

"I'm tired," I said shortly. "I didn't sleep too well last night."

She didn't press the point, but even if she had I wouldn't have told her anything. To be honest, it wasn't only that I knew she and Dad wouldn't believe me, or that I was afraid of being laughed at and told I was fanciful. No, it was more than that. For some reason I felt *ashamed* of my night-time hauntings and unwilling to confide in anyone, as if they were some kind of guilty secret.

Mum turned to Dad. "If you're going to meet Jen from the station, you'd better take Anna along to help with the luggage. I don't want you straining your back and you know what Jen's like – she never travels light."

Dad grunted. It was a "yes" grunt, accompanied by the brief nod of the head that distinguished it from a "no" grunt.

I was as delighted as Becky that Aunt Jen was coming for Christmas. Life was always more fun with her around. You'd never have guessed she was Dad's sister: they were about as different as two people could possibly be. She had never married, saying she preferred her independence.

As the train drew into the station she was already leaning out of the carriage window, waving to us. This time, I noticed, her hair was red. Not chestnut or auburn but *red*, and done in a mass of tiny frizzed curls. She jumped off the train before it had stopped moving and hugged me, then turned to ask Dad, "Hal dear, how's your poor back?"

"Not too grand." He pecked her awkwardly on the cheek. "Where's your luggage?"

She gasped. "Still on the train! Quick, Anna – give me a hand."

We collected her luggage – three bulging holdalls, one with the zipper undone – and loaded it into the car. She got into the passenger seat beside Dad and I climbed into the back. As we drove through the High Street she turned to me. "So how do you like your new home, Anna?"

"It's okay," I said, guardedly.

"More convenient than the old one, I'll bet! I hope it's got central heating?"

"Yes, it has," I said, "but it doesn't work properly yet. Dad's got to get a man in to fix the boiler."

"Poor Hal." She smiled at him sympathetically. "It must be awful for a practical man like you, not being able to do your own odd jobs around the house."

Dad grunted.

At home she was greeted enthusiastically by Becky. Mum was pleased to see her too. She liked Aunt Jen but found her somewhat unpredictable. Giving her ankle-length trench coat a sideways look, she said, "You'll be sleeping in Anna's room, Jen. She'll show you where it is."

I picked up one of the holdalls and led the way upstairs, Aunt Jen behind me and Becky close on our heels. When I took her into my room she said, "Hey, this is nice. But there's only one bed. Where are you going to sleep?"

"In the box room next door. It's okay," I added quickly, "I wanted a change of scene."

She gave me a puzzled look. "Anna, you do like it here,

don't you? I mean, you're not still hankering after the farm? I know you're a country girl at heart, but — "

"I'm not hankering at all," I interrupted. "It's much better living in a town. Lots of people around."

She looked more puzzled than ever, but before she could say anything more Becky demanded, "Where's my present, Auntie Jen? Is it in one of these bags?"

"I wouldn't be surprised." Smiling, she lifted the smaller, unzipped bag out of Becky's reach. "But you'll have to wait till Christmas morning and see what Santa brings you."

"He came last night," Becky said. "But he didn't leave anything. Anna says it's too soon."

"So it is." She turned to me and lowered her voice. "Is there somewhere I can stow this stuff for the time being, well away from little prying fingers?"

I thought for a moment. "There's the loft . . ."

"That'll do. Is it easy to get into?"

"Yes, there's a pull-down ladder." I took the bag from her, watched with interest by Becky. "I'll put it up for you straight away."

"Thanks. I'd better start unpacking."

This was the first time I'd ventured into the loft at our new house. I put Aunt Jen's holdall next to the other old suitcases and then – well, I couldn't resist it – had a sneaky look inside to see if I could spot the parcel with my name on it. Before I could find it, however, Mum's voice called up from the landing, "Anna, what are you doing up there? Come down at once!"

14

Hastily I abandoned the holdall and started down the steps.

Mum was standing at the bottom, her face white with anxiety. "You know you're not supposed to go up into the loft."

"That was in the old house," I pointed out. "It's much easier here because of the ladder."

"That's not the point . . ."

Aunt Jen appeared from my bedroom, followed by Becky. "Please don't blame her, Margaret. It's my fault – I asked her to put my bag somewhere safe. I didn't know she wasn't allowed up there."

Mum bit her lip. "Climbing ladders is always dangerous. Anna should know that."

"I don't think it's dangerous," I said. "It seems perfectly safe to me . . ."

"Don't argue! And in future please do as you're told." Mum turned her back on us and went quickly down the stairs.

Aunt Jen looked at me and I looked at her. Her expression said clearly, *Isn't she rather over-reacting?* Aware of Becky standing between us, staring up at our faces with wide-eyed curiosity, I shrugged and said, "I expect Mum's made us some tea. We'd better go downstairs."

That night I stayed up to play gin rummy with Aunt Jen, and was later than usual going to bed. I had a skimpy wash – there was no hot water again, the boiler was playing up – and got undressed in the box room. That night I didn't feel as scared as I'd expected. Somehow it seemed impossible to think of ghosts when Aunt Jen was around.

The bed was narrow and hard, but I didn't mind. The window was a small one, high up in the wall, and I'd already made sure it was good and shut. In fact I didn't think anyone had opened it since we'd moved in. I sat up, reading: my brain was still too active for sleep. But I felt perfectly calm. I didn't even jump when there was a knock on the door.

"May I come in?" It was Aunt Jen, in flowered silk pyjamas. "We haven't really had a chance to talk yet – not on our own."

That was the best thing about her. She treated me like somebody of her own age who would enjoy a good gossip. I grinned and made room for her to sit on the bed.

She pulled a face. "Good grief! This must be the same mattress they used to give me at the farm. I never slept a wink on it. Anna, are you sure you'll be okay?"

"Yes, of course," I said, trying to sound as if I meant it.

"So, tell me how it is, now that you've moved. You like your new school?"

"Yeah, it's great!"

"And you're making friends?"

"A few." I blushed slightly. "There's a boy called Steven I rather like."

She nodded her approval. "It's about time you had a chance to mix with other kids out of school. The farm was so isolated. It wasn't right for a girl your age, growing up without young company. Apart from Becky, of course – but there's too big an age gap for you to have much in common. You know, I used to worry about you. Sometimes you looked as if you were carrying a great burden on your shoulders." She gave me a probing stare. "In fact you don't seem exactly carefree now. There's nothing troubling you, is there?"

For a brief moment I was tempted to tell her. But I was too used to keeping silent. Besides, although Aunt Jen was quite different in temperament from my parents, I didn't think that she would take ghosts all that seriously either.

I shook my head. "No, nothing. Honestly."

"That's good." She stared round the tiny box-room, then smiled wryly. "Well, I suppose this house is an improvement on the old one, but it still needs an awful lot done to it. Complete redecoration for a start, inside and out."

I felt bound to defend my father. "Dad'll get round to it sometime. We've only just moved in."

"Five weeks ago! The problem is, of course, that he hates the idea of having someone else do the work. He's very bitter about this back trouble and no wonder." She sighed. "I do wish he could talk about it more. That's the trouble with him – and with your mother. They will keep everything bottled up."

I grinned. "Not like you."

"No, nothing like me! I believe in having everything out in the open." Smiling, she got to her feet. "Well, I must let you get your beauty sleep. 'Night, Anna. Shall I switch off your light?"

"No!" I said quickly. There was no bedside lamp in the box-room. I saw the surprise on her face and added, "I want to go on reading for a bit."

"Okay, but better not let your mother catch you."

"I won't," I promised.

She went, and after a while I put my book aside and slid down beneath the quilt. I listened to the sound of my parents getting ready for bed; and then my door opened quietly and Dad's hand came round to switch off the central light. He must have thought I'd fallen asleep. "'Night, Dad!" I called out. He grunted and closed the door.

Darkness.

Darkness and silence.

Well, silence was okay. I could take silence. The longer it went on the better, as far as I was concerned. And it did go on. And on and on. Maybe I was right – Aunt Jen's presence in the house acted as a deterrent. She was too much alive. No self-respecting ghost would dare put in an appearance with her around.

I started to drift into sleep.

Seconds later, or so it seemed, I jerked awake again. Yes, there it was, faintly jingling. The sound of bells, coming steadily nearer, until they were right outside the window. Then they stopped and the tapping began.

It had found me. Moving rooms had made no difference. It knew exactly where I was. Tap, tap. Tap, tap. I sat up in bed, shivering, waiting for what came next.

18

This time the suffocation seemed worse than ever. Mind-crushing. Unbearable. The box-room was small, the walls seemed to be crowding in on me. And it was so airless . . .

I leaped for the window.

It wouldn't open. No amount of pushing and banging would force the catch. Now I knew why it hadn't been opened since we'd moved in – because it was stuck. Another of those jobs Dad hadn't got around to doing – or getting somebody else to do. Now I was trapped, imprisoned, unable to escape.

The sweat ran down my face into the neck of my nightie. My lungs weren't working at all; all I could do was take short, sobbing breaths. I could feel myself losing conscious-ness, sliding down the wall beside the window, until at last I subsided in a shaking, whimpering heap.

Suddenly the door flew open and Aunt Jen stood there. "Anna? I heard banging . . ." She switched on the light and stared down at me. "My God, whatever's wrong?"

"The window's stuck. I can't breathe . . ."

She crouched beside me and put a hand to my forehead. "You're burning up. Do you have a fever?"

"No. But it's so hot in here," I gasped.

Frowning, Aunt Jen pulled me to my feet. "Come and lie down. You must have been having a bad dream."

She made it sound so ordinary, so easily explained, that I could almost believe it. Once again I could breathe normally and the stifling heat had lifted. "Yes," I murmured, as she led me back to the bed. "That's what it was . . . a dream."

When I was back under the quilt she sat down beside me and put her arm round my shoulders. "Anyway, you're safe now. I'm here."

"That's what I thought," I said bitterly. "I thought it wouldn't come now that you're here. But I was wrong."

"What wouldn't come?"

"The— the— " But I couldn't bring myself to say it. Instead I murmured, "The dream."

"Poor Anna." She hugged me tightly. "What was it about?"

"Suffocation," I muttered against her shoulder. "I have this feeling I'm being suffocated."

She held me away from her so that she could look into my face. Her expression was full of concern. "Do you often have nightmares about this?"

Only at Christmas. But I couldn't say that – it would sound too peculiar. Instead I muttered, "No, not often. Only sometimes."

"When did they start? Can you remember?"

"Oh, years ago." I had stopped shaking now. The temperature in the room seemed quite cool again, even cold. "I thought when we moved I wouldn't have them any more. I thought they belonged to the old house. But they came with me."

I was saying "they" when I really meant "it", "it" being the ghost. But if Aunt Jen was thinking in terms of nightmares then I was happy to go along with that. At least it meant I could talk without fear of making a fool of myself.

"Listen," she said. "I'm going to stay with you tonight. I'll bring the mattress in from next door . . ."

"No, it's okay," I said quickly, thinking that if Mum were to find her there she'd be mystified. "It never comes twice in one night. The dream, I mean. Honestly, I'll be all right now. You don't have to worry."

She looked at me doubtfully. "Are you sure?"

"Absolutely."

It took a while to persuade her, but eventually she left me and I settled down again – although still with the light on. It was quite true what I'd told her, about the dream never coming twice in the same night, so I knew I was safe.

But did I mean dream? Or did I mean ghost?

Next morning I overheard Aunt Jen talking to Mum in the kitchen. The hatch into the dining-room was open and they didn't know I was there.

". . . But don't you realise, Margaret, the poor kid's having nightmares about it?"

"That's impossible."

"No, it isn't. I tell you, the human brain is a very strange instrument. Obviously the whole thing is buried deep in her subconscious—"

"For heaven's sake, Jen! You're talking claptrap. Do you think I don't know my own daughter?"

"I think you don't even know yourself. Can't you see it's unnatural, the way you never talk about— ?"

"Be quiet!"

"There you are, you see! I'm not even allowed to mention the subject."

"No, you're not. It's over and done with." Mum's voice sounded shaky. "I don't want you to mention it ever again, do you understand?"

There was a pause. Then Aunt Jen's voice again, her tone quieter and more reasonable. "Oh, Margaret, you're making a terrible mistake. If only you and Hal would talk about it . . . bring it out in the open . . ."

"Jen!"

"Okay, okay." There was a pause, while Mum thumped china about as if to rid herself of her ill-temper. Then Aunt Jen said, "There's just one thing that puzzles me. What is it you've got stored up in that loft you're so keen for no-one to see?"

There was a loud crash. I raced into the kitchen to find Mum staring down at her best cut-glass salad bowl, lying in splinters on the floor. As soon as she saw me she said, "It's all right. I'll soon clear it up. Anna, love, go into the front room and check that Becky's all right. I left her at the table with a colouring book."

I glanced quickly at Aunt Jen. For once her face was as blank as Mum's. "Okay," I said, and went to check on Becky. A hundred times a day Mum would ask me to check on Becky. Sometimes I wondered if this was my main function in life.

In fact Becky was fine, apart from having started to colour

her knee instead of the book. As I cleaned her up I thought of what I'd overheard. Could it be true that something had happened in my childhood – that I was suppressing some awful memory, and that that was why I dreamed about it now? Something to do with suffocation, a childish mishap that I'd never been able to forget? It would explain so much.

"Anna," Becky said in a confidential whisper, "I heard Santa again last night. But he didn't leave anything. Is it tonight that he'll bring my presents?"

I swallowed hard. "Probably," I said.

That was one thing it didn't explain: how, if it was *my* dream, about something that happened in *my* childhood, Becky could hear the bells as well . . .

Later in the day, I found myself alone in the house. Dad had gone to fetch the turkey from the butcher's, and Mum and Aunt Jen to do some last-minute shopping. They took Becky with them and I could have gone too, but I said I'd rather stay at home and finish wrapping my presents.

This was a lie. My presents were already wrapped. What I really wanted to do was take a good look round the loft.

I felt apprehensive as I climbed the ladder. Hidden in one of those suitcases, I felt convinced, was the key that would unlock my memory. But just how shocking a discovery was it likely to be?

In fact most of the cases proved to be empty, the others filled with the sort of rubbish every family accumulates over the years – old clothes, old toys, old photographs. I looked through one of the photo albums, hoping to find something significant, but there were just the usual snaps – Mum and Dad on their wedding day; on their honeymoon in Jersey, looking surprisingly young and carefree; and Becky and me at different ages. In one suitcase I even found my old baby clothes and a pale blue pram cover, embroidered with a large 'A' for Anna. Buried beneath them was a blue-and-white cuddly elephant, and as I pulled it out to take a closer look, I heard a faint, discordant jingle.

I held it up to my ear and shook it. Yes, it must contain a little bell, or several bells – the sort of child's toy you see hanging over a pram. Or a cot . . .

I shook it again.

The sound was uncannily similar. The kind of noise Becky might easily mistake for Santa's sleigh. The kind of noise I heard outside my window . . .

No, it was impossible. I must have been a tiny baby at the time this toy was important to me. Nobody could possibly remember that far back.

And yet . . .

Something stirred in the deepest part of my mind. I *did* remember this toy. The more I looked at it, the more familiar it seemed. Jingle, jingle . . .

A car door slammed. It was Dad, back from the butcher's. Hastily I shut the suitcase and made for the loft entrance, still clutching the blue-and-white elephant. I climbed down to the landing and pushed the steps back into the loft, closing the hatch just as Dad's key turned in the lock.

"Hi, Dad!" I called down the stairs. "Did you get the turkey okay?"

A grunt came from the kitchen.

I went into the box-room and hid the elephant under my pillow. If this toy was haunting me, I had it trapped. Tonight it wouldn't be able to jingle outside my window because it would be safe inside, with me.

I found Dad removing the packaging from the turkey. Watching him, it struck me how strange it was going to be, having our first Christmas in the new house. The farm kitchen had been huge, low-ceilinged and stone-flagged, with a Raeburn stove and a big scrubbed wooden table. Here Dad looked out of place, too large and clumsy for the narrow, space-saving galley.

Curiously I asked, "Dad, do you miss the farm?"

He hesitated, then nodded slowly.

"Especially now it's Christmas?"

He nodded again, and sighed. "Aye, especially now."

"Things always seem . . ." I hesitated, not wanting to say "worse" or "better" because neither was strictly accurate, then continued, ". . . more *important* at Christmas, don't they? I mean, you feel more deeply about things at Christmas."

"Aye," he agreed. "Aye, you do that."

He looked so sad that I added quickly, "But we'll soon get used to it. It's not so bad here, really. In fact I like it."

Without any warning he put his arm around my shoulders and gave me a quick, embarrassed hug. "You're a good girl, Anna."

It was about the longest conversation we'd ever had. I felt very happy. And when Mum and Aunt Jen returned with Becky, who by this time was in a state of wild excitement, I found myself looking forward to Christmas with real enthusiasm. Only one more night to get through and then I could start enjoying myself.

One more night . . .

Of course, the most obvious way to find out what I wanted to know would have been to ask Aunt Jen. I had the perfect opportunity when she came to say goodnight to me in the box-room before she went to bed. Looking anxious, she asked, "Now, you will be all right, won't you?"

"Yes, of course." I leaned back against the pillow, feeling the reassuring lump that was the elephant against my back.

"If you have that dream again, give me a yell."

"Thanks, I will."

"It's pretty common, you know. Lots of people dream that they're being suffocated."

"Do they?"

"So I've heard."

She was waiting – she was actually *inviting* me to ask her questions. But I couldn't bring myself to do it. I was afraid of hearing it from somebody else: I would rather remember it myself, if I could. That way it might not come as such a shock.

Somehow I managed to smile at her. "'Night, Aunt Jen."

"'Night, Anna." She bent to kiss me. At the door she hesitated. "Want me to leave the light on?"

"Might as well."

She smiled. "Your mum and dad are already in bed, so no-one will come along and switch it off tonight. You're quite safe." She left the room, closing the door behind her.

Quite safe.

I took the elephant out from under my pillow and looked at it. If only I could remember . . . I shook it and the bells jangled. They sounded much louder in the still of the night. Becky's room was only just across the landing, and her door was always left open. She'd probably think that Santa had come down the chimney and was inside the house.

I sighed and put the elephant back under the pillow.

Quite safe.

Resolutely I turned on my side and tried to sleep. I almost succeeded; in fact I was just beginning to doze off when I heard bells, and for a confused moment thought the sound must be coming from under my pillow.

But it wasn't. It was coming from outside.

I grabbed the elephant and shook it furiously at the window. "Go away!" I muttered. "We don't want you here. Leave us in peace, whoever you are."

Tap tap.

Tap, tap, tap, tap, tap, tap, TAP!

It seemed more urgent than usual. More insistent, as if it were desperate to get my attention. Any moment now, I thought, the suffocation would start; and I clutched the elephant to my chest, as if to prevent it. I knew there was no point in trying to open the window: I'd had a go at it during the day but couldn't make it budge. So I wouldn't be able to get any air. The suffocation would come and this time I would die . . .

Tap, tap, TAP, TAP, TAP!

Be logical, I told myself. The window might not open but the door would. All I had to do was fling it wide and yell for Aunt Jen. But I was paralysed. I couldn't move a muscle.

I stared at the door, willing myself to get out of bed and walk towards it; and as I stared, I saw something grey and filmy creeping underneath, stealing into the room. I closed my eyes and groaned. At last the thing had found a way of reaching me. It had turned itself into some kind of ectoplasm, changing shape so that it could squeeze under doors. And with it came a horrible smell – a smouldering, singeing smell, as if something were on fire . . .

That's when I realised it wasn't ectoplasm. It was *smoke*!

Released from my paralysis, I leapt out of bed and flung open the door. The landing was filled with smoke – and it was coming from Becky's room. I covered my mouth with my hands and charged straight in. All around me was a thick, grey, billowing cloud which would surely suffocate her . . .

Something seemed to snap inside my head. "ANDREW!"

I yelled at the top of my voice, and I pushed forward to the bed – or rather, to where I knew the bed must be – and pulled the small, limp body into my arms. "It's okay," I murmured, "I'm here. I've got you . . ."

But when I turned around I had lost my sense of direction. I kept blundering into things – the end of the bed, the chest-of-drawers, the rocking-horse – until at last I heard someone call my name. Mum's voice, I think. Coughing, I started towards it. Then somebody grabbed my hand and pulled me through the open doorway, somebody else took Becky out of my arms and I was being half-led, half-pushed along the landing and down the stairs.

"The fire . . ." I protested.

"It's all right, love. Your father's dealing with it."

Mum's voice again. It was her arm around my shoulders, comforting and strong. "Is Becky safe?" I asked. "Did I get there in time?"

"She's fine. Look, Aunt Jen's holding her. They're right in front of us."

Downstairs it was blessedly free from smoke. We went into the living-room and Aunt Jen fetched glasses of water for all of us, then went back upstairs to help Dad. I gulped mine down, holding the glass with both hands, and watched Becky sipping at hers. I couldn't take my eyes off her, hardly able to believe she was alive. She sat on Mum's lap, still half asleep: a little tearful, but that was hardly to be wondered at.

"You saved her life," Mum said, staring at me over her head. "That's what you did, Anna love. You saved her life."

The relief was so great I relaxed against the sofa cushions and closed my eyes.

Soon afterwards Dad and Aunt Jen came back downstairs. Both of them had black smudges on their faces. "Everything's under control," Aunt Jen said, her voice shaking a little.

"What caused it?" Mum asked, hugging Becky even closer.

"Teddy bear," Dad said. "Thrown out of bed, landed on the lamp. Kept smouldering. No fire, only smoke."

"It's the smoke that's lethal," Aunt Jen said grimly. "If Anna hadn't given the alarm . . ." They all turned to stare at me.

"Anna," said Mum, then stopped. She started again, "Anna love, why did you call out . . . that name?"

"Andrew," said Aunt Jen. "She called out *Andrew*."

I stared at their faces. Aunt Jen still looked grim, Mum and Dad almost fearful.

"Because he was my brother," I said. "My baby brother, who died . . ."

The floodgates of my memory, already opened a crack, suddenly burst wide.

I went on, "Today I found his baby clothes, only I thought they were mine because there was an 'A' on the pram-cover . . . and his elephant toy, that jingles when you shake it. I should have known they weren't mine. They were pale blue . . . and anyway mine were all passed on to Becky. But all these years you've kept Andrew's hidden away . . . *and never once mentioned his name*!"

Aunt Jen flashed a look at Mum that said, What did I tell you?

"That's why I had to save Becky," I muttered. "To put things right."

"Put what right?" Aunt Jen demanded.

"What I did to Andrew." I raised my head again, the tears streaming down my face. "It was me that killed him. It was all my fault . . ."

"No!" She moved swiftly to my side, putting both arms around me. "It was a cot death. These things happen, nobody knows why. What on earth gave you the idea that it was your fault?"

"Because nobody would speak to me. That's how I knew they were blaming me for it."

"You see!" Aunt Jen glared at Mum, her eyes blazing. "You see the damage it's done, just because you wouldn't talk about it? This child got it into her head that you held her responsible, even though she could have had nothing to do with it. Good grief, she was only *four years old* – the same age Becky is now!"

Mum stared at me, horror in her face. "I didn't real-ise . . ."

"No wonder she's been having nightmares!" Aunt Jen, now she had started, was relentless. "Dreaming of being suffocated, desperate for air . . . well, it doesn't take a psychiatrist to work that one out. Suppressed guilt, all these years . . ."

"Aunt Jen, please . . ." My voice cracked.

31

"And all because you won't mention that baby's name. *Andrew!*" She almost shouted the word; then suddenly seemed to come to her senses, as if she had shocked even herself. Her voice was quieter when she spoke again. "His name was Andrew."

And Mum said softly, like someone in a dream. "Andrew . . ."

It was quite extraordinary, what happened then. I felt a sense of peace come over the whole house, despite what had happened earlier, and in the distance I heard – so faintly that it might have been my imagination – the jangling of bells, as if someone had picked up the blue-and-white elephant under my pillow and shaken it.

Becky, half-asleep on Mum's lap, murmured, "There's Santa. Did you hear?"

But it was clear from their faces that nobody else had heard. Only Becky and me. I said, "I'm tired. I'd like to go back to bed now."

Mum nodded. "Anna's right. High time we all went back to bed. Becky will have to come in with us. Hal, you'd better go and get cleaned up. You too, Jen. Heavens, it's nearly midnight."

Everything was calm. Everything back to normal. Except that when I went to kiss Dad goodnight he murmured in my ear, "He was a grand lad, our little Andrew. Thought the world of his big sister. You were the one he smiled for, every time you came near."

"Mum used to say it was wind," I said; and gave him a hug.

At the top of the stairs Mum, carrying a sleeping Becky, came to see me into bed. "Anna, love, I'm so sorry. I never dreamed—"

"It's okay," I said quickly, to stop her. I took the toy from under my pillow and put it into her hands. "Look, why don't we give this to Becky tomorrow, to make up for her losing her teddy? I think she'd like it. And I think Andrew would like her to have it."

She took the toy, then kissed me and went hurriedly out of my room.

Aunt Jen came up to say goodnight, the soot cleaned from her face. "You should see the mess that room's in! Now Hal will *have* to redecorate. And while he's about it I've told him to fit smoke detectors."

"You'd better sit down," I said. "There's something I have to tell you."

She listened intently as I told her about the bells outside the window and the tapping, which at last made sense to me. "I think Andrew wanted to get my attention," I said. "Especially tonight. He must have known Becky was in danger and tried to warn me."

Aunt Jen spoke slowly. "I can believe that. Poor little kid, he must have felt shut out. All these years, his very existence denied by his own family."

The thought of it made me want to cry. "Tonight I actually told him to go away . . . that we didn't want him here. Oh, Aunt Jen, how *could* I?"

"Now don't start reproaching yourself. We've let him back in again now and that must make him very happy. In fact, my guess is that you won't be hearing any bells outside your window from now on."

I felt certain she was right. "Now I know why Mum's always sending me to check that Becky's okay." I slid beneath the bedclothes. "Poor Mum, it must have been terrible for her – especially happening at Christmas, of all times."

Aunt Jen looked at me in surprise. "But it didn't. It happened in October."

I stared at her. "Then why do I always hear him at Christmas?"

"Makes sense to me," she said with a shrug. "If you were a child shut out by your family, wouldn't you try to get back to them at Christmas?"

At that moment the church clock struck midnight and the bells began to peal.

THE WOODMAN'S ENIGMA

Garry Kilworth

hey played a game called *Enigmas*: riddles which they would normally do on their home computer. Since they were on a train, they had to play against each other, one inventing an unusual situation, the other making intelligent guesses as to how that situation came about. The game was a puzzle, often a murder, which the second player had to solve.

"I've got one," said Colin. "Romeo and Juliet are lying dead on the floor in a pool of liquid. They're surrounded by broken glass. What's happened?"

His ten-year-old sister Jill snorted, "That's an *old* one, Colin. Romeo and Juliet are goldfish, the liquid is water, and the bits of glass are their smashed goldfish bowl." She flicked her blonde pony tail. "Think of a *new* one."

Colin, fair-haired and tall for thirteen years of age, sighed and stared out of the window at the falling snow.

"I can't," he said. "Not any more. I've run out of ideas. We really need the computer for a good enigma. I don't expect Uncle Giles to have one. He's sixty-something."

The train stopped at Basildon New Town, and the pair of them stared out of the window at the brightly lit streets, full of shoppers and excited children. Christmas decorations were everywhere. In the main square was a giant fir tree, covered with coloured lights. They could hear carols being sung over the square's speaker system.

The train moved on, towards Rochford, their destination. In contrast to Basildon, the countryside around was black and forbidding, a sparsely populated area of few lights. They were used to streets full of people, the noise of traffic, and the hum of the city. They knew that Rochford was an Essex rural district and not at all like their home at Finsbury Park in London. As if that wasn't bad enough, their Uncle Giles lived in a place outside Rochford, a small village called Ashingdon, which sounded like the ends of the earth.

The train at last pulled into Rochford station. They stepped from the carriage onto the powdery whiteness underfoot and looked around them. It was dark and the lights along the platform made a weak show against the night. It was so quiet they could hear themselves walking, even though their footsteps were deadened by the snow.

"Five o'clock in the evening, and it looks as though everyone's gone to bed," grumbled Colin.

Christmas was only seven days away, and here they were in a strange place, with no real celebration to look forward to. Both of them felt pretty miserable, but they knew they had to make the best of an unfortunate time.

"Is that Uncle Giles?" said Jill, pointing to a man in a heavy overcoat just near the station exit.

"I don't know," replied her brother, gripping their suit-case. "We'd better go and ask."

By the time they reached the exit, however, the person had gone. They passed through the ticket barrier and found themselves on a road which sloped down to the town below. Everywhere was soft with new snow. There was no car waiting outside. In fact, the area looked quite deserted.

Colin felt responsible for his younger sister, though in truth he knew she was just as capable as he was in an emergency.

"I'd better phone the cottage. He may have got the times of the trains wrong, and still be at home," said Colin. "You look after the suitcase, Jill."

He found some coins in his pocket and went to the telephone booth, near the taxi stand. Their mother had written their Uncle Giles's number on a slip of paper, and Colin dialled it, only to find that the phone at the other end rang several times without being answered.

Just as he left the booth, a taxi arrived. The driver took out a newspaper and began to read it by the light from the courtesy lamp above his rear-view mirror. Colin studied the man's face for a few moments before walking across to the vehicle. The driver wound down his window and Colin spoke to him.

"Excuse me, could you tell me how much it costs to go to Chase Cottage, Ashingdon?"

"Giles Foster's place? Three pounds." The taxi driver looked at Colin quizzically. "You want to go there?"

Colin shivered, looked at the dark town, then made a sudden decision. There were still fluffs of snow in the air and it was getting colder. There were ice beards on the window sills of the houses. He decided it was best that the two of them got to the cottage as soon as possible. Out in the country the wind seemed harder and sharper than it did in London.

"Yes please," he told the driver, "me and my sister. She's over there. I'll call her. *Jill*! Come on, we're taking a taxi . . ."

They drove out of the town towards the nearby village of Ashingdon, leaving most of the houses and lights behind them. Colin caught a last glimpse of a family crowded around their television set, the colours flickering behind the glass panes, and then the road disappeared into blackness. They could have been anywhere: in the middle of a forest, a desert, a marshland. The headlights of the car only picked out the ruts of car wheels in the snow and the occasional whitened hedgerow.

The taxi driver asked them if they had expected to be met by someone at the station.

"Yes, we were, but our Uncle Giles must have got the times of the trains wrong," said Jill. "He should have been there, but he wasn't."

Colin saw the taxi driver frown in the rear-view mirror.

"That doesn't sound like Giles Foster," he said. "Your Uncle and me go way back, and I've always found him punctual."

Colin shrugged. "Anybody can make a mistake, I suppose," he said. "We've never actually met Uncle Giles – not so's we can remember. Our mum's sick in hospital. She's got to have an operation so she had someone call Uncle Giles and he said he would take us for Christmas."

"What about your dad?" asked the driver, peering out into the blackness as they wound along a country lane. The snow had started falling heavily again now, and large white flakes were flying into the windscreen, some sticking there. The wipers were having to work hard to keep the driver's vision clear.

"Dad's not with us," answered Colin, reluctant to let this stranger into his family affairs.

The car suddenly pulled off the main road and went jolting along what must have been a mud track, through some stark trees which jumped at them out of the head-lights. Tangled thickets narrowed the width of the track the further they went in and a feeling of apprehension went through Colin. He suddenly had the chilling thought that maybe the taxi driver was kidnapping them, and realised how foolish he had been to just jump into the car without checking with the station staff first. Maybe he thought their dad was rich, and would pay a lot of money to get them back again?

"Where are we going?" Colin said sharply.

The driver did not seem put out by his tone, but sounded surprised.

"Chase Cottage. That was where you asked for, wasn't it? Here it is now."

They pulled up outside a wooden shiplap cottage and Colin let out a little sigh of relief. In the headlights he could see that it was a shambling one-storey dwelling, with some rooms in the roof. At least, there were windows up there, and he assumed these were bedrooms. All around the cottage, and at the back, there were sinister-looking crooked trees.

Blackthorns, thought Colin, remembering the word from his Uncle's letter to his mother.

There was only a faint glow of light coming from the front windows, but he was anxious to get indoors now, out of the cold, out of the night. The driver took the suitcase from the boot of the car, and propped it against the picket fence. When Colin held out the three coins for him to take, the man said, "No, I'll sort that out with Giles in a minute. I want to make sure he's home first – it don't look much like it . . ."

Just then a call came over the taxi's radio and the driver found he was being asked to pick up an urgent fare from another location.

"Look," he said, "if your Uncle's not there you'll find the key under the mat. Go in and get warm. I'll come back later to make sure you're all right."

"Thank you," said Jill, and gave him one of her famous smiles that showed most of her gums as well as her teeth.

"Yeah, thanks," said Colin, feeling a little guilty now that he had misjudged the man, though he knew it was always best to be wary of strangers, whoever they were.

The car drove away, its headlights sweeping the thickets in a horizontal arc as the driver did a complete turn, leaving them with the cottage. Once the lights had gone, the place looked very gloomy and forbidding. Still, there was that glow from inside the cottage, which held a promise if nothing else. Jill began to drag the case down the snow-covered pathway, saying, "I can manage, I can manage," when Colin protested.

"You can manage," grumbled Colin, his breath coming out in ghostly plumes, "but will we have any suitcase left when you get there?"

Still, he knew better than to argue with his sister, who was sharper-witted than him in many ways, and he ran forward and tried the front door.

It was indeed locked.

There was a lion's head iron knocker on the door. It was ice cold to the touch, and stiff, but he hammered with this for at least a minute. The sound echoed through the cottage. No one answered. Finally, Jill found the doormat under the snow and lifted it. Underneath there was the rusty key, as well as the corpses of a few summer bugs.

"You can have the dead bodies," she said, "and I'll have the key."

"Thanks very much, sis!" Colin said sarcastically, and was faintly pleased when she couldn't turn the key in the lock, and had to let him try. Unfortunately it didn't work for Colin either. The lock had frozen and they had to take turns to huff warm breath into it for a few moments before the mechanism would budge.

Finally they got the door open and pulled the heavy suitcase in. It felt warm inside, as though someone had not long left the room. Colin pulled off his woollen gloves.

"Hello! Uncle Giles!" Colin called.

No answer.

Strange smells hit Colin's nostrils, of musty furniture and old-person's carpets and curtains. Great Uncle Giles was a bachelor and their mother had warned them the place might not be entirely wholesome. Still, in the dim light this room looked reasonably uncluttered.

The glow they had seen through the window was coming from an open fire in the living-room.

Jill tried the light switch, but nothing happened.

"Just our luck!" she said. "A power cut or something."

"Doesn't matter," Colin replied. "We'll just have to wait until it comes back on. Even if Uncle *has* got a home computer, it won't work without electricity."

"Might have a gas one," said Jill, jokingly.

Colin looked around the living-room, his eyes becoming used to the dim light of the fire. What he saw did not encourage any hope of his Uncle owning a computer. Old dusty books lined two of the walls, and a sepia photograph of young men sitting on chairs under a palm tree hung on the third. The table, writing bureau and Welsh dresser looked dark brown and gleamed with an ancient light: an old person's furniture. The carpet looked as if it had come from the floor of an Indian takeaway. Even the television looked as if it had been thrown away before Colin was born and someone had fished it off the junk heap and got it working again.

"I very much doubt it though, sis. Not even a steam-driven one by the looks of it. We'll have to forget our plan for a while."

The *plan* was that they invent a new video game in order to make themselves enough money to get their father home. Dad was in Saudi Arabia, working for a petroleum company. He had been unable to find work in England, and wanted to make his fortune out in the Middle East, so that he could open a bicycle shop.

The *plan* was not really a pipe dream. Colin and Jill were indeed whizz kids when it came to home computers, and had been playing video games since they were six. It was just another step to inventing one themselves. A sixteen-year-old friend of theirs had set up a workshop in his garage, and was well on the way to producing his third video game for sale in the shops. Though they had sold reasonably well due to lack of competition, his games so far had been pretty mediocre. He was a businessman, not an inventor. His ideas lacked the flair and imagination that he knew Jill and Colin could give a game. If Jill and Colin could come up with a really good one, he had told them, they could make a fortune between them.

"You invent the game and I'll produce and market it," the boy had told them. "We'll split the profits three ways."

So, the two of them had to come up with a brilliant idea, but that would be difficult without a home computer to work on.

Something shifted in the grate and Jill jumped.

"What was that?" she whispered.

Colin stared at his sister's face, shining in the dying light, and knew she would hate it if they were left in total darkness. It was a weird house. The silence was continually broken by the creaks and groans of the timber-framed cottage, and the whistling of the wind around the chimney pot. From the mantelpiece came the slow tick-tock of a clock shaped like Napoleon's hat.

"It's nothing," he told her. "The logs on the fire just moved."

"Why?" came the sensible question from Jill.

"Well, I dunno. Because they're burning away, I suppose."

"They're going to go out soon, if we don't get some more," said Jill. "There don't seem to be any in the fireplace. You go and have a look in the kitchen for some. Maybe you'll find a torch in there."

Colin went to an open doorway leading off the living-room and stared into a solid wall of blackness beyond.

"Is this the kitchen?" he asked, after a while.

Jill retorted, "How would I know? Go in and find out."

"*You* go in and find out. What am I supposed to do? Feel around the floor?"

He left the doorway and went back to the fire.

"Where on earth's Uncle Giles got to? Do you think something's happened to him? Maybe he had a crash in his car, ran off the road in the bad weather, or something?"

Jill said, "There's nothing we can do. We'll just have to wait until he comes home – or the taxi driver comes back."

"We could phone the police," said Colin.

"Let's wait a bit longer," suggested Jill. "We've only been here a little while. One of us could go outside and look for some wood – you can see a bit better out of doors."

"Stay here then," said Colin, going to the front door.

The clock chimed once, on the half hour, and Jill was visibly startled.

"No way!" she replied, coming up behind him fast. "I'm not staying in this spooky place on my own. I think the furniture is alive. If you watch that dresser for long enough it starts to shuffle forward."

"Imagination," Colin said.

"It doesn't matter what it is, I don't like it."

So they both went outside, where it was indeed a little lighter than it had been indoors. A bitterly cold wind cut around the corner of the cottage. There were icicle fringes around the gutters, which glittered in the starlight. Every so often a patch of snow from the roof slithered to the ground.

They went round the house once, looking for a wood-store, but failed to find anything.

"Let's try the trees around the side. Maybe we can find some broken branches or something," suggested Jill.

The now deep snow softened their footfalls, as they went into the spinney and began looking around for lumps in the whiteness. Most of the trees were blackthorns, which not only got in their way, but were too skinny to be of any use on the fire. Then they came to a massive evergreen tree whose boughs were weighted down with snow, so that some of them touched the ground.

The snow had been too heavy for one old dead branch. It had snapped away under the strain, and had fallen to the earth, where it had made a branch-shaped hole.

"Help me carry this to the house," said Colin softly.

"Okay," Jill said very quietly, "but why are we speaking like this?"

It was true, he had started the whispering. It was a reaction to the blackthorn thicket and the tangled briars that joined them together, almost as if they were making a net to trap unwary travellers. There was no real reason for such a feeling. All he knew was that he felt very uneasy, as if someone were watching them from close by, noting their activities.

He stared into the knitted shapes created by the black-thorns, but though he saw many different kinds of darkness there, he could make out no definite forms. It was simply a network of shades and shadows, under the starlight. A fox coughed into the night from somewhere nearby and Colin almost turned and ran.

"I don't like this place much," he muttered, gritting his teeth.

Jill said, "Who does? Come on, let's get this branch on the fire."

Once they had the bough back at the house they realised they would have to break it in half to get it on the fire, so Colin put the fat end in the gap between the gate and its post, and pushed on it until it snapped and sent him flying forwards into the snow. He jumped to his feet quickly and looked around him, half expecting a laugh to come from out of the darkness. There was still that sensation that he was being followed.

"Stop messing about," said Jill.

"I'm not— Oh, never mind."

He didn't want to tell her he was jittery, because that would make her scared too, and he could only just handle himself at the moment. Besides, although he felt so uneasy about his surroundings, he hated to look a fool.

They took the two halves of the branch back into the cottage and luckily managed to fit the pieces on the fire. The logs immediately began spurting coloured gases which burned green and blue. There was an instant flare, though, which helped to brighten the room. Shadows danced around the whitewashed walls, leaping out from some solid objects and slipping under others. The only trouble was that the logs tended to crackle and spit a little, sending smouldering bits of bark flying into the stone fireplace. Colin realised they would have to watch the fire closely in case one of the glowing bits reached the carpet. It wouldn't do to burn down Uncle Giles's cottage for him.

The next thought that occurred to him was that they ought to secure the place properly. If they had been followed from the thicket, then they needed to lock the front door. He found a bolt and shot it home.

Once they were locked inside he felt safer, though there was still that eerie atmosphere in the room, a sort of anticipation, as if the cottage were expecting someone to visit. Colin found himself looking over his shoulder at the door, while he warmed his hands by the fire.

Jill left the fire and began inspecting the room. She came across a large carved wooden chest, undoubtedly from the same Indian takeaway as the carpet. She tapped it with her foot.

"I read a story once," she said, "where a girl got locked in a chest, playing hide-and-seek. They never found her and they didn't lift the lid for a hundred years. When someone did, there was nothing but a skeleton inside, all crouched up . . ."

"You're a cheerful sort," grumbled Colin.

Jill said, "Why don't we open it, and look inside?"

Colin knew that Jill was testing him. He marched over to the trunk, and before she could stop him he threw back the lid. They both took their time before sneaking a look inside, only to see with some relief that it was full of blankets.

"Satisfied?" he asked.

"I knew it was blankets all the time," said Jill.

They went and sat by the fire.

A short while later the silence was interrupted by a sharp rat-a-tat on the front door. Someone was tapping with the knocker, though not at all firmly. It was almost as if the caller felt he might be disturbing the occupants by knocking at all.

Colin looked into his sister's eyes.

"Shall we answer it?" he whispered, having a reason now to keep his voice low.

He received a wide-eyed look and a shrug of the shoulders.

Colin bit his lip and remained still. The knock came again, this time even more gently. Then a voice cried, "Let me in. I know you're in there, the pair of you. You've bolted me out." It sounded like a man with a country dialect.

"Who are you?" cried Jill, her voice wavering.

The reply was muffled, as if the person outside were swathed in a scarf, or had their head down deep in their coat collar.

"Giles Foster."

Colin let out a breath of relief.

"Uncle Giles!" he said, and unbolted the door.

A few moments later a tall thin gentleman stood before them, his eyes red and rheumy and his face pale.

"It's bitter cold out there," he said, loosening the long scarf around his neck a little. He didn't take it off but removed a black hat from his head. "Sharp – sharp as a woodman's axe. I hate the winter when it cuts into my bones like this. You," he pointed at Colin, "and you," a long finger was directed at Jill, "you're children – you don't feel the cold, not like us old 'uns. Bolt the door again, will you?"

Colin did as he was told, ramming the huge bolt into its slot.

Giles Foster went immediately to the fire and sat in the overstuffed armchair at its side.

"I'll keep my coat on for a while," he said, "until I've warmed through. I'm chilled to the marrer. Not much meat there to keep out the winds these days."

And indeed, he did look thin and haggard, his scrawny neck disappearing down into the rolls of woollen scarf. His cheeks were hollow and pinched, and the bones stuck out like points just below the outer corners of his red-rimmed eyes. There was a weary look about him, as if he were attempting to conquer some wasting illness, and losing the fight.

"Give me your hand, girl," he ordered, and grasped her palm, "and yours too, boy."

The thin fingers were like frozen marble.

Jill pulled away sharply, but to cover her bad manners remarked, "You *are* cold!"

"People," replied Giles, "of my age feel it worse than children. I once thought I shouldn't mind being old, that it would be quite comfortable, but it won't be I'm sure. It'll be damned *un*comfortable, especially in weather like this.

50

Now, where was we?" He let go of Colin's fingers and stared into the fire, rubbing his hands together with a pebbly sound. He looked intently at the hissing logs, one of which was burning quite strongly now, and seemed to lose himself in thought for a few minutes.

Colin said, "We had to take a taxi from Rochford station because you weren't there to meet us, Uncle. The taxi man said he would come back, to sort things out with you."

"Ah, did he now? Did he now? Yes, yes, I were at Hockley railway station myself. Ashingdon village is a-tween the two stations you see, and I expected you at that one. Still, never mind. You're here now, and no harm done." His eyes shone brightly from the depths of his narrow face as he peered at the children. "No harm done. You had no bad encounters, I trust?"

"Encounters?" asked Jill.

Giles turned his head quickly.

"Yes, with the ghost . . ."

Colin swallowed hard and his toes suddenly developed pins and needles. Almost without thinking, because he really didn't want to know, he asked, "What ghost?"

Giles studied first him and then Jill.

"Of course," he said at length, "you won't know about our ghost. I don't suppose nobody has told you, has they? Well, we have one, that's a common known fact. He haunts the spinney mostly, but he sometimes comes in here, look-ing . . ."

"Who?" said Jill, excitedly. "Who's he looking for?"

"Not for nobody in particlar. For a way to leave this earth, that's for what."

Colin tried to change the subject, not because phantoms and spooks worried him, because he, well he only *half* believed in such things, but because it seemed to excite their Uncle. Giles's face changed, became feverishly animated when he was speaking. It was almost as if the word 'ghost' inflamed his imagination. His eyes became too bright, his lips quivered, and his expression was more frightening than what he was actually saying.

"The lights have gone," Colin said, in order to change the subject. "Maybe it's a fuse or something."

Giles stared at him for a moment in the firelight, remarked "Light?" and then pointed to the Welsh dresser.

"There's some candlesticks in there, lad. On the shelf under the plates. Bring them here."

Colin went to the dresser, and sure enough, there were two half-burned candles lying on the shelf. He brought them to the fire and lit them on one of the logs. He then placed the two lighted sticks, one either end of the mantelpiece, in the ornate brass candleholders that were fixed on brackets to the wall. The added light made the room a little more comforting, but when he took a look at the expression on his sister's face, Colin realised the talk of apparitions was not over. Jill was fascinated by ghosts, even though she claimed there were no such things.

"We didn't see any ghosts when we were in the spinney," she said to Giles.

He looked at them quickly.

"You was in the spinney? What, *my* spinney? You went out there, in the *dark*? Wasn't you afraid?"

"No," said Jill, sitting on the mat before the blazing logs and hugging her knees. "We don't believe in ghosts."

"Don't believe in ghosts?" snapped Giles, and for a minute he looked quite angry. His eyes shocked Colin and he almost put an arm around his sister to protect her, but then Giles shook his head slowly. A sad expression gradually replaced the stern look.

Suddenly, the logs on the fire spat a shower of sparks into the fireplace. Giles sat up straight and pointed.

"What's that?" he cried.

"What?" asked Colin nervously.

"Them logs – where did they come from?"

Jill said, "*We* got them, from under that big tree in the spinney. What's the matter, Uncle?"

"The big tree in the spinney," repeated Giles, still staring into the flames of the spitting logs. "The old yew tree." He looked across at them with his red-rimmed eyes. "No wonder."

He was silent for a moment, then he continued.

"Yews is ancient trees. They know all the secrets. They can live to more than a thousand years, those greeners. That one's only half such an age. Still and all," he played with a button on his overcoat, "it means you'll meet the ghost, that much is certain."

Both children glanced nervously towards the front door,

despite their conviction that spectres were simply inventions of an over-imaginative mind.

"Why do you say that?" Colin asked Giles. "There's no such thing as ghosts really, is there?"

"You've spoke on that once already," replied their Uncle, using a poker to stir the logs, and getting another shower of sparks for his trouble. "Them what repeat things really don't mean what they says. They usually mean the opposite.

"Let me speak more on this ghost, and then you can make up your own minds."

Giles coughed once, and then told the tale.

"The years was fiddling a bit, working round to finishing off the century. There were this woodman, a fine figure of a man. He cut trees like some folks cut butter. Thought it time to lay aside his axe and go courting, settle a bit. He'd been coppicing, pollarding and cutting down trees all his life, and had reached an age when his muscles and bones complained in bed of a night. Coppicing and pollarding, well, they're special ways of trimming trees, so that they send out more growth. A sort of pruning. But the cutting down of trees, that's a different story."

Uncle Giles's cheeks grew waxy in the firelight as he talked and his eyes had a faraway look to them.

"You see in them days they didn't do much in the way of replanting, and the woodmen over the centuries had all but destroyed the forest, leaving only a copse or two, a thicket or three. Some say the old yew tree killed him of a purpose, while he were on his way to the church . . ."

"Killed him on purpose?" repeated Jill. "You mean the yew tree attacked him?"

"Nothing so theatre-like as that, I'm sorry to report. There he were, all dressed up in his best togs, when he walked under the old yew. He were on his way to a carol service, just a few days before Christmas.

"He never arrived at the carols, though several folks was expecting him. So once all the singing were done, they went out looking for him. They didn't need to go far. He were close nearby, hanging by his neck. Somebody walked under the old yew, caught a clip on his ear from a dangling boot. When he looked up, there were the woodman, gripped by the throat in the fork of a branch, swinging backards and forrards as easy as a dead rabbit on a string.

"Since that time he's been wandering the spinney, haunting the people who own Chase Cottage, making a nuisance of himself every time someone burns a piece of the yew that took his life . . ."

Colin cried, "That's why he's coming tonight? Because we burned a branch of the yew?"

"That's the reason," said Giles. "People don't do it that often, you see, being as yew don't burn too well. It spits and sparks, and those who know about kindling and firewood never use yew in their grates. It's the woodman's only chance to send his spirit to rest."

"Why?" asked Jill. "Why is it his only chance?"

Giles stopped, and stared into the flames.

"What is it?" asked Jill.

55

He pointed with a lean finger.

"I do believe that might be the very branch that strangled the woodman, though of course I can't be sure. Dead as a weasel on a fence, he were, and doomed to roam what were left of the forest he had cut down with his axe. There were no going straight to heaven, of course, because the woodman was not in particlar a religious man. The way of his death were very mysterious, as you can see, and until someone living guesses exactly *how* the woodman met his death, his spirit is not to be put to rest.

"In those days people knew about ghosts, and when he started appearing before the owners of the cottage, there were much thought put to the question of his death. Some of the best brains in the village came up with ideas, from suicide to murder, but failed to reach the answer right. These days no one cares any more, and wouldn't know what to do if they did."

"That's a terrible story," said Jill, sitting down at the old man's feet. "And so the woodman has to keep coming back as a ghost until someone guesses how he was killed? Come on, Colin – we can think of how he died, the way we play *Enigmas*!"

Colin didn't feel much like playing games, but sighed an agreement, to please her.

Giles nodded slowly, but added, "I feel I have to warn you that if you fail to get the right answer, there is a penalty."

"What?" asked Colin, his skin tingling with fright.

"The woodman's ghost will return, night after night, and

harass you until you're half out of your mind with fear. And when you think you can't be scared no more, he'll strike your soul with such terror that you'll wake up in the morning dreading the coming of the dark."

The children could see that their Uncle was deadly serious, that this had become more than a game – but there was a compulsion to go on that neither of them could resist, even though they were more scared than they had ever been in their lives before.

Jill swallowed hard and said, "Did the wind sweep the branch down low and scoop him up?"

"Doubtful," said Colin, seeing the disapproval on his Uncle's features. "It would have to be a pretty strong wind. Can we ask you questions, Uncle?"

"You can try," replied Giles.

"Right! Now, did the woodman climb the tree?"

"Yes, he climbed the tree."

"And slipped!" cried Jill.

"Possible," replied Giles, "but *why* did he climb the tree in the first place?"

Colin considered this. He and Jill were used to playing enigma games on their home computer, so it was just a matter of getting rid of the *impossibles* to come up with a *probable*.

"It was Christmas," muttered Colin, "and the yew is an evergreen, I know that much, so he was climbing up to get fir cones."

Giles shook his head in contempt.

"Although the yew is an evergreen it bears scarlet berries, not cones. You know very little about trees, boy. Have you learned nothing in your life?"

Jill, who loved elaborate wild guesses, said emphatically, "There was a kite caught in the branches and the woodman wanted to take it home to his grandchildren, so he climbed up to get it."

"Wrong again. The woodman were a bachelor."

Colin muttered thoughtfully, "An old bachelor?"

"Growing on, you might say," said Giles, a little testily, "but not *too* set in his ways."

"So he wouldn't have a girlfriend, would he? He wasn't climbing up to break off a few small branches, to make some sort bouquet, or something?" Something struck Colin as being very likely. "Maybe he was going to help decorate the church?" he cried.

"Why wouldn't he have a lady friend?" said Giles stiffly. "There were still a little sap in his bones. He may very well have had a lady for which he carried an affection. As for decorating the church, you'd catch him dead first. He just weren't the sort. He were a rough and ready sort of fellow, not a flower decorator."

Jill said carefully, "Now, this girlfriend of his. She was at church, wasn't she? Otherwise he wouldn't be going there. You said he wasn't very religious, so why else would he be going to a carol service?"

Giles clasped his hands together, and for the first time his eyes showed approval.

"Good lass, good lass."

"So," said Colin, frowning, "he was on his way to church to see his girlfriend – though they were both quite old – and he wanted to take her some firewood as a present . . ."

"You've forgot that yew don't burn well. This man were a woodman who knew on such things."

"I like the idea of him having a girlfriend," said Jill. "It's romantic. Did she like *him* much?"

"Ah, there's the tragedy. No, not a great deal. She were one of them spinsters, you see, who thought on men as idle layabouts. He once tried to kiss her, on the cheek of course, and she give him short shrift."

Colin remembered trying the same thing on a girl at a recent birthday party. "You need an excuse for that sort of thing, when they don't want you to do it . . ."

"An excuse," repeated Jill, slowly. "He wasn't taking her a bunch of anything, because you said so. What's up a yew tree? Nothing but yew berries and branches, surely?"

"Maybe a bit of ivy," said Colin.

"A bit of ivy!" cried Giles. "What sort of ivy?"

Colin was puzzled.

"Are there different kinds?"

He received a slow, encouraging nod.

"Lots of climbing creepers in them woods out there – all sorts if you think on it."

Jill suddenly sat up straight and clicked her fingers. All attention switched to her. She laughed.

"Got it!" she cried.

Giles and Colin both stared at her.

"Have you?" said Giles.

"What then?" said Colin, sceptically.

Jill beamed at them, a little smugness showing through her smile.

"Mistletoe!" she said. "It's a creeper, like ivy, isn't it? He was climbing up the tree to get some mistletoe, so that he would have an excuse to kiss the spinster, and he slipped and fell, getting caught in the fork of the branch."

Giles coughed and stirred the logs once more with the poker. The fire hissed at him, blue and green smoke flaring from within the logs, and he gave it a jab. There was a peaceful look on his face.

"At last," he said in a voice full of intense satisfaction. "At long last. The woodman's ghost be able to close his eyes and go to his rest."

The three of them sat there, as the candles burned down slowly, and the yew logs spat angrily into the fireplace. On the mantelpiece Napoleon's hat ticked away, deepening the silence in the room. Colin's heartbeats seemed to be keeping time with the old clock. He was wondering why their Uncle was playing this game of silence with them. He looked as though he was waiting for something. What did he expect them to do?

Suddenly Giles sat bolt upright in his chair and cocked his head as though listening to the night.

"Listen!" he said.

Then he pointed a boney finger at the door. There was an expression of triumph on his face. The children immediately guessed that the ghost was coming.

Jill went quite pale.

"Stop it!" she said. "You're frightening me."

"Ah," said Giles, "but you don't believe in ghosts, remember? All you have to do is tell him you know the answer to the riddle, and he'll go away, won't he?"

Colin jumped to his feet and ran to the side window, the one that looked onto the spinney. He pulled the curtain back with one hand and peered out into the night. The panes of glass were frosted over and the snow piled into the corners, but as he stared into the darkness, he saw a figure, a dark shape, coming slowly through the trees towards the front of the house. The figure was having great difficulty with the blackthorns, that hooked at his coat with their thorns.

Colin gave a cry and stepped back from the window, letting the curtain fall back into place.

"What is it?" said Jill in a strangled voice. "What is it?"

"Some— somebody's coming," said Colin.

They heard a crack from just beyond the gate, as if someone had trodden on a twig.

Jill went to the front window now, looked out, and then stepped back from the panes just as Colin had done.

"A man, dressed in black," she whispered.

"Black?" cried Giles. "Ah, people get buried in black.

61

The woodman wore black, for visiting the choirmistress. He were a sober man, who took his courting seriously."

The gate creaked as it was opened, then clicked shut. When he listened very hard, Colin could hear the squeak of snow under someone's leather soles. The footsteps came up to the door of the cottage and then halted.

"What's happening?" asked Jill who had now gone over to the other side of the room, as far as possible from the door. "What's he doing? He can't get in, can he? He's a wood ghost. He can't get into houses."

There was a scrabbling sound at the lock, as if someone were fitting a key.

"This used to be the woodman's home, you see," said Giles, "so he has his own key. This were his cottage which is why there's no escape from him, in here. He can come and go as he pleases . . ."

The lock clicked back and the door handle turned but nothing happened. Then the creature outside rattled the door back and forth, as if trying to force an entry. The door held fast.

"He can't come in," said Colin softly. "I bolted the door, remember?"

Silence followed, then a tapping at the window pane.

Colin went to the window and peered through the narrow gap where the curtains met. He could see a dark, hunched figure looking back at him with strange, warped eyes. The face which held those eyes was distorted by the ice that had formed in a layer over the panes.

Garry Kilworth

Colin stepped back again, sharply this time.

The sound of snow squeaking, then a hammering on the door.

Giles tutted.

"You'll have to let him in, you know. He won't go away. Why don't you open the door? I can't do it. It has to be you." He smiled, his mouth a curve of red on his pale features. "You don't believe in ghosts anyway."

Colin knew he had to do something. His heart was pounding in his chest and his fingers shaking. What if he were to let the ghost in? What was the worst that could happen? He felt sure they had guessed correctly how the woodman had died, so he wasn't here to hurt them. He just wanted to be told what they had discovered, so that he could be released from his need to haunt the cottage.

"I'll open the door," he announced, and marched to the bolt, throwing it back before Jill's squeal hit his ears.

The door swung back and an old man stood before them. His face was white and lined, and his eyes colder than winter. He glowered at Colin, holding the boy with his gaze. Jill came across the room to grasp Colin's hand, and they both wilted under the apparition's glare.

"I believe in ghosts," whispered Colin, "I really do. I can tell you how you died. You'll be free. You can stop roaming the spinney."

The ghost stepped inside the cottage doorway and kicked the snow off his shoes.

"What on earth are you talking about, young man?" he

63

said. "What took you so long to answer the door? I'm freezing. Let me get by that fire . . .."

He suddenly reached out and gripped the children by the shoulders, one hand on each.

"Colin and Jill, eh. Yes, I can see the family resemblance. How did you get in?"

"Key," said Jill, "under the mat."

"Ah yes, the key. It's been there so long I'd forgotten I'd put it there."

"Please, woodman . . ." began Colin, but the ghost interrupted him with, "Woodman? What's this *woodman*? I'm your Uncle Giles. The car broke down on the way to the railway station. I've been walking for over an hour. I came over the fields, it's quicker that way and here we are. Sorry I wasn't there to meet you. How did you get here?"

"Taxi," said Colin, faintly.

"Oh, well done! Showed a bit of initiative, eh? I like that in my relations. Who brought you? It was Bert Wilson, wasn't it? He's the only one who knew about the key. Trust him. Memory like an elephant. Well, let's get this door closed." He gave the door a shove with his foot and it slammed shut. "And let's have some light in here, for goodness' sakes." He reached up and turned a switch. The room was suddenly bright.

When Colin and Jill turned to look at the chair by the fire it was, of course, quite empty. The ghost of the woodman had played its final trick on the living, and had gone now to the place where it belonged, in the land of the dead. On the chair where it had been sitting were a few droplets of moisture, as if the material had been touched in passing by a light frost.

"Now," said Uncle Giles, "you mentioned someone called Woodwind or something. What's he, an imaginary pal, eh? Ha, ha! Used to invent my own playmates at your age." He stared at them intently. "Well, perhaps not. You seem a little too old to be playing pretend games."

"We are," said Jill, firmly.

"Yes, thought so. What about this Woodstock chappie, then? Oh, what—" Uncle Giles turned and stared at the spitting yew logs. "Someone's put yew on the fire. Never put a yew log on an open fire," he said, sternly. "It spits." He paused, then added, "Brings the ghost too, but I don't want to frighten you. We'll damp down the fire, and perhaps he won't come."

"You never burn yew logs?" asked Colin.

"Of course not. Haven't I just said so?"

Jill nodded at her brother.

"That accounts for it then. He's already been," she said.

"Accounts for what?" asked Uncle Giles, and when he did not receive a reply, went on, "Good lord! You don't mean old Giles has been here?"

Colin said, "*Another* Giles?"

"Yes, Giles Foster, my ancestor and namesake. What am I saying? *Your* ancestor too. Your Great-great Uncle Giles as a matter of fact. Here, was he? Well I'm blowed! He . . . he didn't ask you to solve any riddles, did he?"

65

"He did, and we gave him the right answer," said Jill, proudly. "He won't be haunting the cottage any more."

Their uncle looked at them with some awe.

"Well done, well done! Never dared to have a go myself. He's pestered me every time I mistakenly burned a piece of that yew, but if I had tried to answer the riddle and got it wrong, he would have been in here *every* night."

"Well, now he's gone forever," said Colin.

"I hope you're right. You both seem pretty sure of yourselves. Now, come into the den, I want to show you something I bought today, especially for the pair of you, to make your Christmas with an old man a bit more exciting . . ."

He led them into another room, switching on lights as he did so.

"Tra-la-la!" he cried, gesturing towards a desk.

On it was a brand new home computer.

"Your mother rang me and said it would give you a lot of fun. I don't understand the things myself, but you'll soon sort it out between you, I expect. Now, let me show you your rooms. I expect you're both quite tired after all your ghost-busting. We'll have a cup of cocoa and some biscuits, and then . . ."

Later on, when the house was silent, Colin got up and crept to his sister's room. Her window overlooked the spinney. Together they stared out onto the starlit landscape, at the snow among the white trees. There was a kind of mist out there, weaving its way between the tree trunks. It might have been Old Giles Foster's ghost, having a last look before leaving this world.

"I bet I know what you're thinking," said Jill.

"What?" asked Colin.

Jill gave him one of her gummy smiles.

"We've got our video game, the one that'll make us enough money to get dad home, haven't we?"

Colin thought quickly and luckily it came to him.

"You mean the game called *The Woodman's Enigma*?"

"That's the one!" said Jill.

THE WEEPING MAID

Robert Swindells

y name is Laura, and I have two children. Like most children, mine are fascinated by stories and films about ghosts. Like most parents I want to say to them, "There are no such things as ghosts," but I can't, because of something which happened to me when I was nine.

It happened at Grandma's house, in London. It was a big old house on a tree-shaded avenue in a district which had once been fashionable. Grandma didn't have the whole house – it would have been far too big for her, though her father had owned it all, and his father before him. She had the upstairs part, including some dim little attics which were never used, while some people called Jenkinson lived downstairs and had use of the cellars. I used to love visiting Grandma because she spoiled me, and because there were big empty rooms to explore, and dim corridors and great, dark cupboards you could hide in. I was allowed to go anywhere I chose, except down the stairs which led to the

Jenkinsons' flat. I hardly ever saw the Jenkinsons, because we used different staircases and they were often away on business. It was an exciting house for all sorts of reasons, but the best thing about it was the ghost, and that's what I'm going to tell you about.

The ghost was known as the Weeping Maid, because it wore an old-fashioned housemaid's uniform and was always seen crying. I'd never seen it myself, but I believed in it because Grandma had seen it lots of times and so had Grandad before he died. Mum told me she'd never seen the ghost though she grew up in the house, but I'm afraid I didn't believe her. I suppose she thought I'd be frightened if I knew Grandma's house was haunted, but I wasn't. Ghosts never hurt you. It's other people who do that.

Anyway, that autumn when I was nine my parents had to go away for a few weeks and I was sent to stay with Grandma. It was the longest visit I'd ever made and it was in termtime too, so I was really happy. No school, and three weeks in which to poke about and look for the Weeping Maid. The day I arrived I asked Grandma if she thought I'd see the ghost this time. "Do you want to?" she asked, and when I nodded eagerly she murmured, "Why, for Heaven's sake?"

"I want to ask her why she weeps," I replied, and Grandma shook her head and said, "You're an odd child, Laura. Lively, intelligent and pretty, but definitely odd."

I was there two weeks before I saw the ghost. Two weeks and two days to be exact. Every day I patrolled the shadowy landings and wandered through the big cold rooms where the furniture was draped in great white sheets which made chairs and beds and tables look spooky and somehow menacing. I peered into cupboards whose doors squealed when I opened them, and whipped aside long curtains which looked as though somebody might be hiding behind them. The one thing I didn't do was climb the narrow, creaky staircase which led to the attics. This staircase was dark and twisty, and the three tiny rooms under the roof had remained unvisited for so long that generations of spiders had strung their webs across the stair, though what they caught in them I don't know: it was far too cold for flies. Anyway, I didn't go up because I didn't fancy breaking through those dusty, ancient webs, some of which must have been spun by spiders long since dead.

One day – it was late afternoon and beginning to get dark – I was walking along the landing which led past the foot of the attic stairs when I thought I heard someone sobbing. I stopped, holding my breath, and listened – there it was, quite faint but definitely real. It seemed to be coming from the staircase. I stood absolutely still while my heart pounded and a prickly sensation crept up the back of my neck and over the top of my head. For years I'd longed to meet the Weeping Maid yet now, with the moment surely at hand, I was frightened. Perhaps I'd never truly believed. I don't know. I can only say that I stood for a long time listening before I gathered the courage to tiptoe forward and peer into the web-furred gloom.

It was halfway up, sitting hunched over with its head in its hands like the picture of Cinderella in a book I had when I was little. Apart from that, and the black and white outfit it wore, it wasn't the least bit as I'd imagined a ghost would be. I'd expected it to be semi-transparent, ethereal, scarcely there at all, but in fact it seemed quite as real, quite as solid as I was myself. I even fancied I could see the effect of its weight on the step it was sitting on, though it couldn't have weighed much, even in life. I'd expected a grown woman, but the Weeping Maid was frail and tiny with wrists and ankles like a child's. I couldn't imagine it ever having coped with the sort of back-breaking drudgery which was once the housemaid's lot. The poor creature was so slight, and sobbed so piteously that pity overcame fear and I said, "What is it, Miss? Can I help you in any way?"

As I spoke, the sobbing stopped and the ghost raised its head, gazing down at me through red-rimmed, puffy eyes. It didn't speak, but I heard a thin, hoarse whisper inside my head. "It's you. You. At last." A faint smile seemed to cross the thin white face and the ghost stood up, making no sound. It beckoned with a bony finger then turned and climbed the stairs, which did not creak. The webs remained unbroken where it passed, and these were the only proofs I had that this maid did not live.

I followed, making the staircase squeal, and the webs stretched and snapped and clung as I ascended, but I didn't mind. It was a sort of trance, I think. I was not afraid, only intrigued. As I climbed, I asked my question, but not with my voice. I asked inside my head, "Why do you weep?" and the voice I'd heard before said, "I will show you. Follow me."

The room was very small, and contained nothing except a battered horsehair sofa. It was cold, and the only light came through the cracked, grimy skylight set in its sloping ceiling. Through this I could see the darkening sky, and I knew that down below tea would soon be ready and Grandma would be waiting.

Without speaking, the ghost indicated that I should sit down. There we were, the Weeping Maid and myself, sitting at either end of a horsehair sofa in a bare little attic at half past four on a dull afternoon in October. I was not afraid. As I said before, I think it was a sort of trance. I sat looking at her, and she gazed into her lap where her thin pale hands lay folded, and I was going to say she told me her story, but that's not really true. She didn't say a word, yet her dreadful tale unfolded before me as though I was watching a play.

It was 1914. The maid's name was Alice, and she was fifteen years old. She had two brothers and three sisters, all younger than herself, who lived with their parents in a village many miles away. Alice had been sent to work in this house because her family was poor and needed her wages. She had been here about a year, and she shared this tiny attic with another housemaid, an older girl called Sarah. Alice was homesick and found the work terribly hard, but

Sarah was a good friend, and there was somebody else too: Bertie, the fishmonger's lad, who came with the fish on Friday mornings and had taken a shine to Alice. Sometimes, if she wasn't busy elsewhere, Alice was able to dally for a minute or two with Bertie by the kitchen door, and she would long for her half-day, which was Tuesday, when they would meet secretly and walk together in the park. Secretly, because a maid who was seen walking out with a boy could be dismissed without a reference and would never work in service again. Both Alice and Bertie knew of girls who had been forced into the workhouse or onto the streets after losing their jobs in this way.

Alice's employers – the family who owned the house – were called Bertram. The Bertrams had only one child, a handsome lad of twenty named Geoffrey, who held a commission in the Guards and was often away from home. Geoffrey had recently married and his pretty wife, whose name was Laetitia, lived in the house too. The Bertrams were good employers – strict but fair – and Mrs Alloway, the Housekeeper, had told Alice she was lucky to be in service with them. Whenever she was feeling unhappy, Alice tried to remember this.

It was in August of that year that the Great War broke out and everything changed. War is a terrible thing, of course – everybody knows that – but it caused great excitement in 1914. Stability is fine but it gets monotonous, and people tend to welcome anything which disrupts routine and brings a bit of variety into their lives. Day after day that summer, the newspapers carried blood-curdling accounts of German atrocities, and young men rushed to enlist in Kitchener's army. Red, white and blue bunting blossomed in dingy streets and the summer air throbbed to the sound of marching bands.

Young Geoffrey Bertram – Lieutenant Bertram – shared the general mood of festivity as his regiment prepared for embarkation, but his parents had mixed feelings. It is one thing to see one's only child commissioned in a fashionable regiment in peacetime, and quite another to watch him march away to war. People die in battle, and junior officers tend to be particularly vulnerable. However, the Bertrams were patriots who knew where their duty lay, and so they pushed their anxieties to one side and put preparations in hand to give their son the best possible send-off.

There was to be a party: a magnificent affair for more than a hundred guests, on the night before the regiment sailed for France. For a week beforehand, every servant in the house was hard at work scrubbing, dusting, burnishing. Outside, the gardener and his boy toiled to bring lawns, flowerbeds and borders to a peak of perfection. Like everybody else, Alice worked from dawn to dark. Her Tuesday half-day was cancelled, and as she slaved she consoled herself by thinking about the minutes she might steal with Bertie on Friday. But there was one thing she didn't know – by Friday Bertie would be a soldier too.

*   *   *

At this point there was a pause – a break in the play or vision or whatever it was I was experiencing. 1914 faded away and I was in the attic, on the sofa, gazing at the frail phantom who had covered her face with her hands and was crying softly. A long time seemed to have passed, yet the light was the same as before and I heard no voice below, calling. I felt a surge of tenderness for the creature beside me, whom I could no longer think of as "it", and I went to touch her shoulder as a mute way of saying, "You are not quite alone. I am here." But when I stretched out my hand it went into her, finding nothing tangible on which to rest. It was as though I'd reached for a rainbow.

After a while the crying stopped and the maid resumed her voiceless narration.

She almost didn't see Bertie that Friday. When he came whistling along the side of the house with his basket, Alice was kneeling before the hearth in a remote bedroom, scrubbing the grate with black lead. She knew it must be time for his visit, but tonight was the night of the party and the room wasn't half ready. Her heart ached, but she didn't dare abandon her task. She'd resigned herself to not seeing him when the door opened and Sarah tiptoed in, grinning.

"He's coming," she whispered. "I heard his whistle and his boots on the gravel like soldiers marching. Do you not want to see him?"

"Oh, Sarah!" she cried. "You know I do, but –"

"Then hurry up, silly, or he'll be gone. I'll finish this."

How she'd hurried! Scurrying along the landing, praying not to bump into the Housekeeper or the Butler or anyone who might delay her or send her about her business. Flying down the backstairs, arriving at the kitchen door just as Mrs Edgeley was closing it in her sweetheart's face. "Oh, Cook!" she cried. "One minute, please. Only a minute." And she said it with such a pleading look, and Mrs Edgeley was so soft-hearted, that she got her minute, which was to prove infinitely more precious than she could know.

"I've something to tell you," he said, and she knew straight away what it was. "I've enlisted. We leave in the morning for Salisbury Plain."

"Why, Bertie?" Pain in her eyes. "I thought you cared for me."

"Oh, I do Lissie, really I do." Lissie was his name for her. "Only – well, they need all the men they can get and everybody seems to be going. I can't spend the whole war being the fishmonger's boy while other lads're –"

"Dying?"

"Fighting. Fighting for me, Lissie. You do understand, don't you?"

She understood. "Meet me," he urged. "After work. God knows when we'll see each other again."

She shook her head. "I don't know, Bertie. There's a big do tonight. A hundred guests. I don't know if I'll get away."

"You worked your half-day, Lissie. Tell 'em your beau's off for a soldier, then they're sure to let you go."

"It's not that simple, Bertie. They don't even know I have a beau. I'll try. That's all I can say."

"You'll be there, Lissie. Five past seven, under our tree."

So confident. So sure. And so they'd parted. A brief goodbye. Till tonight.

She'd gone straight away to Mrs Alloway and asked. One hour, Ma'am. Half an hour. Please? The Housekeeper, dubious, had approached the Butler, who had mentioned it to the Master, who had passed it on to the Mistress, who said no. "Tonight of all nights," she said, preoccupied with tender thoughts of her son. "It's out of the question, of course."

She wasn't a cruel woman, the Mistress. Partly, it was the fact that this child – this Alice – had evidently been seeing a young man on the sly, but mostly it was a mother's natural concern that everything should be perfect for what might well – heaven forbid – be her boy's last party.

And so young Geoffrey had his send-off, and Bertie did not.

And Alice? She performed her duties to the best of her ability and kept her feelings to herself. What else could she do? She didn't forget, though. It was one of those things you don't forget, which lie inside and slowly fester till they infect even the sweetest of natures. And so it was with Alice.

And how did I come to know all of this? I don't know. As I have said, the ghost didn't speak, and we never left the horsehair sofa. I sat there while scene after scene unfolded in front of me and the voices came from inside my head. And I seemed to know how Alice had felt all those years ago. As I watched the events of her sad, brief life I think a part of me became Alice, because when I saw how Bertie marched away, I cried.

And now there came an interruption. The unfolding had stopped – perhaps because of my crying – and it had not resumed when I heard Grandma call. I looked at Alice. "I – I'm sorry," I whispered. "I have to go now." I saw the faint smile I'd seen on the stairs, and the voice in my head murmured, "Tomorrow?" It was a question. I nodded. "Tomorrow," I whispered, and that was a promise.

"Wherever have you been?" cried Grandma, as I walked into her sitting room. "Just look at the state of you!" I looked in the mirror over the mantelpiece and saw my skirt and cardigan grey with dust, and a veil of webs in my hair. I told her I'd been into the attics, and she shook her head and tutted and made me wash and change while tea waited.

When we finally sat down she said, "What on earth were you doing up there, Laura?" I took a sip of my tea and gazed at her through the steam. "Sitting with the Weeping Maid," I said. "She's called Alice and she used to work here."

Grandma smiled. "Really? And did you ask her why she weeps?"

"Yes."

"And what did she say?" I knew from the way she spoke

that Grandma didn't believe me. She thought I was playing a game and she'd decided to join in.

"She hasn't told me yet," I said. "But her life was very sad. She was only fifteen and she had to work like a slave and hardly ever saw her family."

Grandma nodded. "The life of a servant was hard in those days, Laura. What else did she say?"

"She loved a boy called Bertie," I told her. "But he went off to war and she couldn't even say goodbye because of Geoffrey's party. Geoffrey was off to the war too, you see."

Grandma looked at me. There was a funny look on her face. "Geoffrey?" she said. "Who was Geoffrey, Laura?"

"Geoffrey Bertram, Grandma. His people lived here, and so did Laetitia, his wife."

She nodded. "I know. Geoffrey and Laetitia Bertram were my parents and your great-grandparents, Laura, but I didn't realise you knew so much about your ancestors. Has your mother been speaking to you about them?"

I shook my head. "No, Grandma. It was Alice. I – didn't know they were my ancestors, though. I think something awful's going to happen."

Grandma frowned. "Whatever do you mean, child?"

"Well," I said. "Bertie went away and Alice was very upset but she wouldn't still be weeping, would she? Not about that. Something worse must have happened. Perhaps he never came back."

Grandma was looking at me in a very odd sort of way. "Laura," she said, softly, "I know that many children have highly developed imaginations, but yours is something to be wondered at. It is prodigious, and it frightens me. Would you mind very much if we talked about something else now?"

I did mind, because my head was full of Alice and her unfinished story, but I said I didn't and we talked about school and friends and that sort of thing till all the muffins had gone and the teapot was empty. And all the time, I knew Grandma was thinking about something else. I hadn't meant to worry her, but I could tell she was thinking about Alice and Bertie and Geoffrey, and a time before she was born. I think she knew now that I wasn't playing a game. Perhaps she wished I was.

And me? I couldn't wait for tomorrow.

I was at the foot of the attic stairs before nine the next morning. It was a wet, blustery day and as I stood there, gazing up through the shadows I could hear the rattle of raindrops on the skylight and the wind booming and racketing about the gable. I climbed the creaking stairs, feeling far more afraid than I had yesterday, and peeped into the attic. Nobody was on the horsehair sofa. There was a small puddle where rain had seeped through the crack in the skylight and dripped onto the floorboards. Otherwise the room was empty.

I didn't know what to do. Perhaps there's a way of summoning ghosts but I didn't know how. I whispered

"Alice" a few times, but nothing happened. I looked into the other two attics but they were completely bare. I went downstairs and wandered from room to room opening cupboards, pulling faces at myself in dusty mirrors, squinting through rain-spattered windows. Perhaps the voice which had whispered "Tomorrow" had meant the same time tomorrow. I'd try again in late afternoon.

Grandma occupied three rooms – well, two rooms and a tiny kitchen really – at one end of the house. At the other end, as far away from her quarters as you could go, were two rooms which connected, with a really tiny room between them which you walked through to get from one to the other. These were my favourite rooms, because I could do anything I liked in them without Grandma popping up unexpectedly, which she sometimes did elsewhere. It was about a quarter to ten and I was in the first of these rooms when I thought I saw something move in the tiny connecting room. I went over and looked in but nobody was there. The door which led to the other room was closed. I twisted the knob and pushed and there she was, standing in the middle of the room. The same shadow of a smile, and the voice in my head said, "This is where it happened."

"What?" I asked, looking at her, but she indicated a window-seat which had doubled as a linen-chest and we sat down. I had slipped into yesterday's trance-like state, and the maid's tale continued as if there had been no interruption.

* * *

82

The war, which most people had thought would be over by Christmas, dragged on into 1915. Its novelty was wearing thin. The daily papers carried long casualty lists and there were shortages. In the Bertram household, life went on much as before except that most of its members, above stairs and below, knew somebody fighting at the front and were perpetually anxious, even when they weren't aware of their anxiety. The appearance of a messenger-boy in the street froze everybody's blood till it became clear which house he was heading for, whereupon that house became an isle of misery in a sea of temporary relief. In January one of the footmen, a lad named James, enlisted, and in March came the news that he was dead. A pall of gloom settled on the house. To keep the home fires burning ceased to be an exhilarating challenge, becoming instead a grim duty, stolidly performed.

1915 gave way to 1916. Alice was now seventeen, and had not seen Bertie for two years. There were occasional letters, but Bertie did not write easily and Alice's reading was laboured, so that this method of communication was unsatis-factory except as a way of showing that each was alive and thinking of the other. Then, on a raw November morning in that year came the news Alice had dreaded. It was brought by the lad who had taken Bertie's place at the fishmonger's. He told Mrs Edgeley, who passed it on to the Housekeeper, who sent for Alice.

Alice knew what it was before Mrs Alloway spoke. She saw it in the woman's eyes and backed towards the door, shaking her head, saying "No, no, no," in a tiny, whiny voice. Mrs Alloway nodded and came forward with open arms and Alice fell into them, wailing.

They gave her the rest of the day off. She sat on the narrow, lumpy bed in her room under the eaves and stared at the wall while her fingers plucked at the thin blanket, pleating, smoothing, pleating again. At first she thought about nothing at all, but as the hours wore on she began to remember how they had prevented her seeing him for even half an hour before he marched away, and she rocked herself back and forth on the bed's edge while thin, mewing noises came out of her mouth. Later, when it began to get dark, Mrs Alloway brought warm milk mingled with laudanum, and she and Sarah put Alice to bed, where she slept in Sarah's arms till dawn.

Dawn. A new day, filled with possibilities. The rebirth of the sun, and of hope.

Not for Alice. Not that dawn, nor any one of the thousand which now remained to her. Without Bertie – without the possibility of his return and of their life together – she woke each morning to a despair she found almost unbearable. She did her work mechanically, ate without interest and slept fretfully, slipping in and out of a nightmare world scarcely distinguishable from her waking life. The one hope she harboured was that she might die soon, and in her sleep.

December. The raw wind sucked at her bones and preparations for Christmas mocked her grief. On the fifteenth, she was cleaning a lamp in the library when Sarah came in.

"Cook says you're to come to the kitchen directly, Alice," she said. "Someone's asking for you."

"For me? Who is it?"

"I don't know, dear, but you'd best hurry."

There was no caller in the kitchen. Mrs Edgeley nodded towards the half open door. "He's out there. Wouldn't come in. Make it snappy, girl."

Alice hurried to the door. A soldier was standing on the step. A gaunt, unshaven soldier with haunted eyes and a dirty uniform. He smiled briefly and touched his battered cap. "Miss Milford – Miss Alice Milford?"

"Yes." She was thinking of Bertie and struggling not to cry.

"Biggs, Miss. Herbert Biggs. Pal of Bertie's. He said to give you this if he was – if he was —." The man shrugged apologetically and held out a small, square package wrapped in brown paper and tied with string.

Alice looked at it, then at the soldier. "What is it?"

"Dunno, Miss. It's heavier than it looks. Bertie said you'd know what to do with it. Here." He thrust it at her as though anxious to be rid of the thing. She took it, and it was heavy. The man smiled again. "It's a Christmas-box, Miss. An early Christmas-box, and I'm Santa Claus. I've got to go now, so —"

"Oh, don't go, Mr Biggs. Not yet." Alice took hold of his sleeve to detain him. "Bertie – were you with him when he — when he died?"

"Oh yes, Miss. Close as I am to you now."

"How did it happen? Did he suffer a great deal?"

The soldier shook his head. "Never knew a thing about it, Miss. One minute we was chatting, sharing a fag, and the next he was gone. He was forever talking about you, Miss, and he was a good mate an' all. It's a shame, that's what it is. Bloke like that."

Alice nodded. "Yes. Well. Thank you Mr Biggs for bringing this, and for answering my question. I've wondered, you see."

Biggs nodded. "Bound to, Miss. Only natural. I'll be off now. Goodbye then, and good luck."

Alice carried the little package up to her room, wept over it and hid it, unopened, in her clothes-box. Christmas was pressing, and she must return to her duties.

Thursday was Sarah's half day. As always she would go to her parents at Barnet, returning late. With luck, Alice might get off at six and have the room to herself for a couple of hours. That was when she would undo the package.

It had been a long time since Alice had taken an interest in anything at all, and she waited fretfully for Thursday, praying that her friend's half day might not be cancelled. The day crept round at last, there was no cancellation and at one o'clock Sarah put on her shawl and bonnet and left the house.

Six o'clock. Alice, weary but excited in a sad sort of way, climbed the creaking stairs to the cold little room in the eaves. She lit a candle, opened the clothes-box and took out the package. Sitting down on her bed, she began to pick with trembling fingers at the knots her sweetheart had tied. Presently the old grey string fell away and Alice unfolded the thick, crackly paper to reveal a sturdy cardboard box with a lid. She stroked the box with her fingertips, crying softly, knowing his fingers had touched it too. After a time she pulled a rag from the pocket of her smock, dabbed her eyes, blew her nose and lifted the lid. Inside was a Mills bomb and a folded bit of paper.

She sat for a while with the box in her lap, gazing at the bomb which gleamed in the light from the candle. Then she smoothed out the scrap of paper and tilted it towards the light.

It was only four lines, done in pencil. Alice's lips moved as she read the words. It was a rhyme. It said:

> *Lay his fire*
> *Sound his knell*
> *Send him off*
> *Without farewell*

Knell. Alice had frowned over that word. She knew what it meant, but it wasn't a word Bertie would use. He'd never been one for fancy language, nor poetry neither. Who had helped him then – Herbert Biggs?

The message was clear enough, and the maid's heart thumped as she hastily re-wrapped the package. There was a loose floorboard under the bed where Alice kept her few small treasures and she hid it there, replacing the board carefully, blowing fluff and dust over it for good measure. There are secrets and secrets, and this one she knew was lethal.

Alice rose next morning with a glint in her eye and a purpose in her heart. Mrs Alloway noted the change and told herself the child must be getting over the loss of her beau at last. The Housekeeper was a gentle soul, and Alice's apparent improvement made her feel happy all day.

Christmas came and went; a somewhat sombre celebration because of the war which seemed destined to go on for ever. At the front, junior officers died like flies and promotion was rapid for those who survived. Young Geoffrey Bertram was one of these. He had distinguished himself in action, and at twenty-three was already a Major. In the summer of 1917 his parents received news which gladdened their hearts. Their son was to get home leave, after which he would report to Staff College. If he did well there, he would pass out as a Staff Officer and his days at the front would be over.

He came home in October; thinner, older – far older – but alive. The Master had assembled the entire household staff at the front door, and as his son's taxi turned into the driveway they cheered. Alice joined in, and nobody noticed how she trembled as the young man waved and smiled.

She did it on a chill night, one week later. Geoffrey had gone with the Master to his club and was not expected back till late.

Mrs Alloway said, "Alice, you are to lay a fire in Master Bertram's room so that he can put a match to it if he feels the cold."

"Yes, Ma'am." Alice sketched a bob and hurried away, and the Housekeeper gazed after her for a moment, puzzled by the flicker of fear she fancied she'd seen in the maid's eyes.

Alice stood the bomb on its base-plate on the grate and built a pyre of sticks and crumpled newspaper round it, watching the door as she worked. When the bomb was quite invisible she placed nuggets of coal among the sticks and paper, leaving plenty of spaces for the draught to circulate. When the fire was laid she filled the scuttle, swept the hearth and left, closing the door behind her. She felt sick with fear, but she bit her lower lip and thought of Bertie.

Waiting was the worst part. Sarah and Alice retired at nine, and Alice lay on her back with her eyes open while her friend dropped off beside her and slept like a log.

It was a terrible thing she was doing. Terrible. She thought about Laetitia. Sweet, pretty Laetitia; how she would grieve. The Master too of course, and the Mistress. They were so happy now, and soon they'd be so, so sad. They'd feel as she had felt, which was only fair, wasn't it? Well, wasn't it? Anyway, she was doing what Bertie wanted her to do, and that was her sacred duty, wasn't it – to carry out her beau's last wish?

More than once she was on the point of getting up, of slipping down the dark stairs and along the landings to undo what she'd done, but she didn't. She waited, damp and tense, watching the phantom floating shapes, listening.

What would it be like, the explosion? Perhaps it'll blow the whole house up, then we'll all be out of our misery, won't we? No. Bertie wouldn't have asked her to do this if it was going to kill everybody, including herself. Bertie would know.

What if they suspect me, afterwards? What if Sarah lifted the floorboard when I wasn't here and saw the bomb? Or what if Herbert Biggs tells on me? They'd hang me, wouldn't they? I'd be a murderess. I am a murderess.

She moaned and sat up, swinging her legs out of bed. Sarah stirred, muttering, "What is it, Alice? What's up?" Alice froze, and as she waited for her friend to settle she heard a door bang far below. It was too late. They were back.

She lay, cold with horror, straining to hear. Doors. Footfalls. Sudden laughter. A cough. She could go down, even now. Confess. Show them what she'd done and throw herself on their mercy. She'd be dismissed, of course. Without a character. They might get the police, and then what? Prison? The madhouse? She moaned, jerking her head from side to side on the pillow, and then thought, fear and for a moment consciousness itself were obliterated by the awesome blast which ripped through the house below.

I heard that explosion. Felt it. An explosion which had

happened more than seventy years before. I even had its acrid stench in my nostrils. How the ghost did that: how she communicated these things to me so vividly I'll never know. The phantom detonation brought me to myself for a moment and I knew I was sharing that window seat with my great grandfather's murderess. I suppose I ought to have felt outrage, revulsion, but I didn't. I gazed at the frail spectre and felt only pity.

The rest was quickly told. She'd tumbled out of bed with exclamations of feigned alarm and joined the other servants on the stairs. The upper part of the house was full of the smoke which poured from Master Geoffrey's room, the door of which had been blasted outward to hang by a twisted hinge across the landing. The room itself was wrecked and burning, and it was immediately obvious that the occupant had not survived.

The master had taken control, urging the near-hysterical staff to form a human chain which fought the blaze with buckets of water till the fire brigade arrived. Everybody assumed an air raid was in progress and that the house had sustained a direct hit.

Later, it emerged that there had been no air raid. Experts who examined Master Geoffrey's room concluded that the young officer had brought home a bomb as a souvenir from the front, and that this had accidentally exploded. It was, they said, a fairly common occurrence.

The Bertrams mourned. Laetitia, expecting a child, was prostrate with grief. The house became a place of shock and of sadness as its occupants strove in their several ways to cope with the disaster.

And Alice? Did she glory in her deed? Had Geoffrey's death made up somehow for Bertie's, as she had thought it would? Now that it was obvious she would never be suspected, did her solemn expression conceal a heart filled with savage satisfaction?

No. In the days and weeks which followed, the maid's state of mind deteriorated. She wandered through the house sighing, shaking her head and muttering to herself. She wouldn't go near Geoffrey's room, even after repairs had been carried out. Sent that way on an errand, she would make elaborate detours to avoid the scene. As she brooded over the terrible thing she had done, she began to doubt her own sanity. The shadow of the madhouse haunted her dreams. She grew thin, pale and silent.

The war ended, but the celebrations which followed meant nothing to the maid. She yearned to flee this house in which she could never know a moment's peace, though peace had come to the world. She planned to seek another situation, but before she could act on her plan she was struck down by the influenza which was then raging across Europe.

In her cold little attic, dying, she laboured over a note to the Master in which she confessed her crime and begged forgiveness. This note she entrusted to Sarah, exhorting her to take it to Mrs Alloway at once. Sarah, horrified by the note's contents and distraught at Alice's approaching death, could not bring herself to do this. Instead, she put the note in a cigarette tin, which she concealed behind a loose brick near the copper boiler in the wash cellar. She meant to deliver the note later, when her friend was safely in her grave, but the influenza took Sarah too, and the note remained hidden.

I saw the copper. It was the last picture to pass before my eyes before the whole thing faded. When I came out of my trance I was alone, but I knew what I had to do. I had to go down to the cellar – the Jenkinsons' cellar – and find the loose brick. The tin would still be there, with the note inside. I must take it to Grandma, and tell the maid's story. I must tell it in such a way that Grandma would feel sorry for Alice, as I did myself, and forgive her.

And that is exactly what I did. The Jenkinsons were away, so getting into the cellar wasn't difficult. The copper was as I'd seen it in my trance, except that now it was festooned with cobwebs. The loose brick was still loose, but rust had sealed the cigarette tin, so that I had to bang it on the flags before I could get the lid off.

It gave me an odd feeling, seeing Alice's cramped and faded script. There wasn't enough light in the cellar to read by, so I crept up the forbidden staircase and took the letter to my room. Even then I couldn't make it all out, but I read enough to know it was Alice's confession.

Grandma didn't know what to do. She'd convinced herself I'd made up the maid's story from stuff Mum had told me, and now she was faced with the letter. I could tell she wanted to think I'd forged it, but she couldn't. The rusty tin, thick yellowed paper and faded ink were conclusive. She listened to my story, but she never told me whether or not she was prepared to forgive poor Alice.

I was disappointed at the time, but I understand now. After all, young Geoffrey was her father – a father she'd never known – and I've heard it said her mother, Laetitia, was never quite well again after the tragedy, so Grandma had a great deal to forgive. It must have taken some thinking about. She's gone now, of course, so I'll never know for certain, but I think she must have forgiven Alice, because Grandma's house is my home now – mine and my children's – and none of us has ever seen the Weeping Maid.

I know she did a terrible thing, but I like to think Alice is with her Bertie now, in a place where nobody ever hurts anybody else, not even by accident, because everybody knows how easy it is to hurt, and to be hurt.

A place where if somebody is weeping, somebody is sure to ask them why.

THE INVESTIGATORS

David Belbin

hen his parents finally left, Mark Sullivan sat down on an upturned tea-chest, took a deep breath, and surveyed his new kingdom. He had one large room, a tiny kitchen and, downstairs, a bathroom which he shared with two other people. As his mother had pointed out more than once, it was a grotty flat. If Mark had managed better exam grades, and got into his first-choice polytechnic, he would be in a clean, warm hall of residence now. Instead, he was on the top floor of a crumbling Victorian terrace, with nothing but cobwebs for company.

Dad was a builder. He had assured Mark that the building was sound, even if it looked decrepit. The window frames were rotten and it would be cold in winter, but at least there was no damp. Mark wasn't so sure. He looked at the peeling pink paint on the walls. Who in their right mind painted a wall pink? And there was a smell that he couldn't identify – a deep, earthy, slightly disturbing smell. Cooked cabbage? Old socks? It didn't bear thinking about. The agency said that the flat had been left empty for some time because of an "oversight". Mark thought it more likely that no-one had been willing to rent it.

Through the open window, Mark heard children's excited voices. He remembered noticing a Junior school round the corner on Forest Road. It must be lunch time. The children's distant babble was relaxing, making him feel more at home. Nevertheless, he closed the window. Smell or no smell, the flat was starting to get very cold. He turned up the gas fire, then lay down on the bed. The iron bedstead was ancient, but the mattress was new and comfortable. He felt his brain going numb. He wasn't used to getting up early in the morning – not since the exams back in June.

Three-quarters of an hour later, Mark woke with a start. For a few seconds he didn't know where he was. The room was stiflingly warm. He turned off the gas fire. He tried to think. Something had woken him up. Perhaps someone had knocked. He opened the door and looked down the stairwell.

"Hello?"

Nothing. Nobody. Leaving the door on the latch, Mark went down to the bathroom and used the toilet. The stairway was rather steep and had one of those timed light switches that went off after half a minute. Coming out of the bathroom, he couldn't work out where the switch was. The landing had no window and, even in daytime, it was very gloomy. He fumbled his way back up the stairs, holding on to the banister. There was no carpet and each stair creaked, the sound echoing through the house. If anyone tried to burgle him in the night, he thought, he was bound to hear them coming.

It was Friday. Term didn't start until Monday. Mark emptied his rucksack, put on his quilted jacket, and walked down the three flights of stairs which took him out of the house. The last thing his dad had done was to slip him fifty quid "until your grant cheque's in", so that he could buy decorating materials. He walked up the Alfreton road until he found a shop which had a sign saying 'cheapest paint in Nottingham'. He came out ten minutes later, rucksack crammed with ten litres of magnolia paint, a can of white gloss, and several rolls of woodchip paper.

Mark didn't finish decorating until late on Sunday night. He sat on the floor, huddled in front of the gas fire, watching a film. He had to sit right on top of the fire, as the window was half open to let out the smell of two coats of paint. He'd brought the ancient portable telly and video from his room in Southampton. Now that he'd moved, he knew, the telly wasn't licensed. He'd never broken the law before, and felt slightly uncomfortable about it.

There was a knock on the door. Mark panicked. Suppose it was about the TV licence? He turned the telly off and thought about where to hide it. Then he told himself not to be silly. Detector vans didn't work that late on Sunday nights. It was probably someone from one of the downstairs flats. It would be nice to meet a neighbour.

He opened the door. A young couple stood on the landing, each wearing a smart dufflecoat. The man was tall, with a square jaw and receding hairline. He carried a large plastic case. The woman was of average height, but seemed small next to the man. She had wavy brown hair, a pointed nose, and eyes that twinkled.

"Hello," they said in unison.

Mark blinked at them. They couldn't be neighbours, because they had coats on. They looked too old to be ordinary students. Moreover, who called on a stranger this late in the evening?

"I wonder if we could come in?" the woman asked, in a polite voice.

Now Mark knew what they were. He'd been warned before he came. They were religious types – Jehovah's Witnesses or something like that – who tried to get lonely students to join their cult.

"We're not trying to sell you anything," said the man. "Honest."

It was the "honest" that did it. The man's slightly pleading tone made Mark loosen up. The couple looked nice enough. Even if they *were* religious nutters, they couldn't hurt him. And he hadn't talked to anyone for two and a half days. He could use the company.

"I'm sorry," he said to them. "Of course you can come in, as long as you don't mind the smell of paint."

Mark took their coats. Then he closed the window. The couple introduced themselves as Ruth and Ian.

"Are you a student?" Ruth asked Mark.

"Yes. Combined Humanities. I start my course tomorrow."

"Nice job you've done on the flat," Ian said.

"Thanks," said Mark, putting the kettle on. "But aren't you going to tell me why you're here?"

There was a long pause.

"The thing is," Ruth said to him, "we need your help."

"How do you mean?"

Ruth looked anxiously at Ian. She was very pretty, Mark thought.

"Are you superstitious?" Ian asked Mark.

Mark shrugged.

"I don't walk under ladders unless I need to, but I wouldn't exactly call myself superstitious. What do you mean?"

Ruth answered.

"Do you believe in ghosts or the supernatural?"

Mark laughed.

"I don't even read my horoscope."

The couple exchanged another glance. They seemed relieved.

"That's all right then," Ian said. "You see, we're paranormal investigators."

Mark cringed. They *were* nutters, after all.

"You mean, like Ghostbusters?"

Ian smiled.

"Not at all. We're academics. Psychology graduates. We're both doing a PhD at UCL."

"UCL?"

"University College, London," Ruth told him. "Under Professor Hugh Jenkinson. He's one of the world's leading figures in paranormal research."

"You mean he believes in ghosts?"

"Not at all," Ian replied. "In fact, most of our department's work consists of proving that so-called hauntings are the work of the imagination or hoaxers. In our field, you have to be a sceptic, or the scientific establishment won't even begin to take you seriously. That's why we needed to know if you believed in ghosts before we tell you our story."

Mark poured the tea.

"What story?"

Ruth looked nervously about the room.

"How long have you been living here?"

"This is my third day."

"Have you noticed anything . . . unusual while you've been here?"

"Not really. I've been too busy painting."

"Any noises in the night?"

Mark shook his head.

"I sleep pretty heavily. Oh, the house makes noises and

the wind rattles the windows a little, but you expect that in an old house, don't you?"

Ian nodded.

"Have you been told anything about the resident before you?"

"No. At least, only that the flat has been empty for a long time because the agents made a mistake."

Ruth laughed.

"A 'mistake'!"

Ian smiled ruefully.

"What actually happened was that the owner refused to let the flat out after the last occupant left."

Mark furrowed his brow.

"Why *did* the last occupant leave?"

Ruth began to speak.

"Because of the . . ."

"No."

Ian put his hand on Ruth's arm to stop her talking.

"We're jumping ahead of ourselves. Mark, if you're willing to listen, I'll tell you the story from the beginning."

Mark was intrigued.

"I'm willing to listen."

Ian began.

"A few years ago, we got a report about a haunting in this house. Now, our department gets reports like that all the time – we can't investigate them all, but we do file them, which was what we did in this case. However, when the professor went to file this report, he found that there were two earlier entries, each several years apart, listing a similar phenomenon."

"What phenomenon?"

"I'll get to that. Now, two reports separated by a number of years isn't so unusual, but three . . . well, that automatically merits an investigation. So the professor came here. Unfortunately, he was too late. The person who'd reported the ghost, a young man like yourself, had moved out. He'd been scared out of his wits.

"The professor tried to get permission to conduct research in the house while the flat was empty, but the owner refused. She told her agents that the flat was not to be let out again, nor were they to allow anybody to visit the flat who might disturb the ghost. She thought she might be liable for any harm that came to them.

"The professor managed to persuade the agents to inform him should the flat ever be offered for rent again, which they did, last week. The lady who used to own this building died recently and the new owner isn't so squeamish. The agents informed Professor Jenkinson and he put us on the case."

He paused. Mark interrupted impatiently.

"Well, what is the case? What scared this bloke so?"

Suddenly Ian got up, his long body moving swiftly over to the flat's small hallway. He opened the door and pointed down the stairwell.

"According to each set of reports, you've got a ghost on your stairs."

Mark stared down the dark stairwell. All he could see was the dingy wooden stairs. He reached out and switched on the light.

"Well, there's no ghost here now."

"Maybe not," said Ruth, "but that doesn't mean there won't be."

He turned round and looked at her. She smiled.

"I thought you were a sceptic," he said.

"Of course I am," Ruth replied. "Neither Ian nor I have seen any definite proof of the existence of the supernatural. But if you're going to be a good scientist, you have to keep an open mind. If you know what results you're looking for before you start, then those are the results you're likely to get. And it has to be said, this stairwell does offer a very promising prospect."

Mark looked again at the stairwell. He hadn't bothered to decorate it. The walls were covered with that horrible pink paint. Even with the light on, the corner at the bottom of the stairs was in shadow. You had to turn the corner and walk a few metres down the corridor to get to the bathroom. If you were a nervous, imaginative type it would be easy to get scared during that short walk. A trick of the light could make a shadow move, and if you were half asleep . . .

Mark closed the door.

"So what do you want me to do then?"

"Nothing."

"Nothing?"

"That's right. Obviously, we'd be interested if you do see or hear anything. Though, for your sake, we hope you don't. You see, another testimony that the ghost on the stairs really exists isn't any use to us. Ghost sightings are ten a penny."

"So what are you after?" Mark asked.

Ian glanced at Ruth. They both spoke together.

"Proof," they said.

Ruth explained.

"Research has shown that there are certain times when astral spirits, or ghosts, or whatever you want to call them, are more likely to manifest themselves. For instance, when there's a full moon."

Mark grimaced.

"I thought that was only in films."

"Actually," said Ian, "a film is what we want to make. We'd like to come here about once a month, and bring some video equipment with us."

"And what would you do?"

Ruth finished her tea before speaking.

"We'd try and disturb you as little as possible, obviously. We'd set up the video camera at the top of the stairs and activate it if we saw anything unusual."

Mark stared at them. They looked perfectly serious but it sounded daft to him.

"So you'll just sit at the top of my stairs waiting for a ghost?"

"That's more or less it," Ian said. "We'll bring a blanket to keep ourselves warm. And a flask, maybe."

"You'll sit there all night?" Mark asked.

"Oh, not all night," Ruth replied. "All the sightings take place at a fairly specific time. Between midnight and one. So we'll arrive late in the evening, then return to London at about one-thirty."

Mark looked at his watch. It was eleven-thirty.

"And I suppose you want to start tonight?"

Ian opened his large case. It contained a lightweight video camera and a tripod.

"If it's all right with you," he said.

In the morning, when he got up, Mark was inclined to dismiss his odd encounter of the previous night as a dream. But there, neatly folded in his small hallway, was the couple's blanket. There were also three upturned mugs on the sink unit.

"So when are you coming again?" he'd asked, before going to bed.

"Can't say for sure," Ruth had replied. "It has to be a last-minute decision, depending on other investigations we're doing and when the conditions are right. We could ring you, if you were on the phone."

"I can't afford to have a phone, I'm afraid."

"Well, in that case," Ian said, "we'll just turn up. We'll be no bother, I can promise you that."

* * *

For a couple of nights, Mark slept badly, half expecting the creak on the stairs, the ghostly screams. But nothing happened. The polytechnic term started, and took up all his time. He'd always found it easy to make friends. Now he nearly forgot about Ruth and Ian. There was only the scribbled phone number of their college, stuck to his pinboard, to remind him that they existed.

Two or three times, Mark told visitors the story of the ghost. But they didn't believe him. They either thought that he was winding them up or that he was trying to scare them. So he forgot about it. There were no ghostly noises in the night, unless you counted the residents of the flat below, whom he never saw, tramping down the corridor and flushing the toilet.

Then, one night in November, he got home late from the pub. Turning the corner to climb up to the fourth floor, he found Ian, camera in hand, blinking down at him.

"Hi!" he said. "I hope you don't mind. The bloke in Flat 1 let us into the house. We told him we were friends come to visit from London, so he let us wait upstairs for you."

They shared a pot of tea before Mark went to bed.

"We got nothing last time," Ruth told him. "Zilch. But tonight ought to be better. There's a full moon."

She gave him a full smile, then her eyes returned to Ian and met his. They were obviously in love, Mark saw. Well,

106

you'd need to be, to spend half the night at the top of a freezing stairwell.

"Tell me," he asked them. "What *exactly* does this ghost *do*?"

Ian reached into his pocket and produced two photocopied sheets.

"I thought you might ask."

The reports were very short. Mark read them.

Geoffrey Williams, a 42-year-old brewery worker, reports being woken in the night by the sound of feet on the stairs leading up to his room in a Nottingham boarding house. On opening the door, he confronted the pale white shape of an elderly man at the top of the stairs. Williams fainted, but woke to the sound of an awful scream. A few weeks later, returning to his room at night, Williams saw the same ghostly figure climbing the stairs. Williams fled, but behind him he could hear awful banging sounds, and the same terrible scream. He moved out that night, and the room has since been unoccupied.

This report was dated 1952. The next was from 1967, when the building had changed from being a boarding house into seven flats.

Kerry Barlow, a model, and her boyfriend, an unemployed musician, were in their top-floor flat one night when they heard banging noises followed by a scream from the landing outside. They opened the door and found nothing.

However, the following night, when Kerry was alone, she heard footsteps on the stairs. Thinking it was her boy-friend, she opened the door. There she saw a white apparition on the stairs, shuffling towards her, moaning. He reached out his arms to her and fell forward. She saw that he had no feet. Terrified, Kerry shut the door in his face. Then, she heard the banging sounds again, followed by a terrible screaming.

Mark put down the report.

"So she moved out too. But other people must have lived here after Kerry Barlow, and before, for that matter. Why are there no reports from them?"

Ruth explained.

"Well, it's possible that none of them saw or heard anything. But you've got to bear in mind that most people who see things only tell their friends about it. They don't report it to the police or contact a university department they don't know exists. They're too scared, or feel foolish. So we never hear about the majority of sightings."

Ian looked at his watch.

"We really need to set the camera up."

He got the tripod out of the case.

"Well, wake me if you see anything," said Mark. "But otherwise leave quietly. I've got a nine-o'clock lecture tomorrow."

He left them in his small hallway, "They're loonies," he

thought as he drifted off to sleep. "Likeable loonies, but loonies all the same."

When Mark got up in the morning, Ruth and Ian were packing away.

"I thought you meant to leave by two?"

"I know," Ruth said, stretching. "But we both thought we saw something, so we hung on in case it happened again."

"And did it?" Mark asked.

"Hard to tell," said Ian. "When you're really tired you're inclined to imagine things. We'll have to analyse the film very carefully when we get back to London."

"After we've had a sleep," added Ruth.

Mark looked at them sympathetically.

"Let me make you some breakfast before you go," he said.

Gratefully, they accepted and sat down.

"How long are you going to keep this investigation up?" Mark asked, as he passed them slices of toast.

"That depends," said Ruth. "Some investigations last for years before they get a result, or are abandoned. But our funding runs out next summer. We have to get our theses written up so that we can get a doctorate, then find a proper job."

"In London?"

"I doubt it," Ruth replied. "Professor Jenkinson's always having trouble with funding. We'll probably have to go to America. They take the supernatural more seriously there."

"And is this the only case you're researching?"

"Oh no!" Ian replied. "We've got nearly a dozen. The department's been looking into some of them since it was set up, eight years ago. But this is one of the most promising."

"Do you mean to say," Mark asked, "that your department's been looking for evidence of ghosts for eight years and still has no proof?"

Ruth nodded.

"We have lots of *evidence*," she told him, "but most of it is open to interpretation. Images that could have been faked, or have an entirely rational explanation. *Proof* is another thing altogether. Mankind has been looking for solid proof of the supernatural for as long as anyone can remember."

"Well, I'm sorry to tell you, but I think you're wasting your time," Mark said.

He saw them to their car, a shiny blue 2CV. "But you're always welcome, anyhow."

He reached into his pocket and handed Ian his spare set of keys.

"Borrow these. Next time you can let yourselves in, make a drink, get warm."

Ian took them gratefully, and shook his hand. It was a beautiful, clear, October day. The air was crisp. Birds sang. The old buildings around them looked impressive in this light – dignified and historical. Ruth held out her hand, then

David Belbin

changed her mind, and kissed Mark on the cheek. Close up, there were lines of tiredness around her eyes. Somehow, they made her even prettier. She got into the car. Both of them waved, then they drove off towards London.

For several days after their second visit, Mark hoped that Ruth or Ian would write to tell him what they'd found on the videotape. But they didn't. He considered phoning UCL. In the end, though, he decided against it. They hadn't promised to contact him, and were probably embarrassed that they'd found nothing at all. However, despite his scepticism, he found himself looking forward to their next visit.

Early in December, Mark's older sister, Penny, gave birth to her first baby, a girl. Mark went back to Southampton for the weekend to see them and the rest of the family. They were glad that he had settled in well, and was enjoying the course. He didn't tell anyone the story of the ghost, in case it worried them. But he did ask his dad a question.

"Is there any reason why someone might raise a staircase?"

"In your house, you mean?"

"Yes."

"Probably dry rot. I told you some of the wood in that house looked dodgy. Raised, you say?"

"Yes. Three or four inches."

"They'll have had to reinforce the floors, make them thicker. Probably did it whenever they converted the house into flats."

Mark remembered that the house had been converted to flats in the late fifties. Now he knew why the ghost had the bottom of his legs missing in the sightings after then. Ruth and Ian would be delighted when he told them.

He got back to the flat late on Sunday night. It was half an hour before he noticed the note, neatly folded on top of Ruth and Ian's blanket.

Hope you don't mind, we finished your milk. No luck at all tonight, but we'll try again. Sorry we missed you. Love, Ruth and Ian.

Mark was disappointed to have missed them. He'd really wanted to tell Ruth and Ian about the moving stairs. It was odd, but Mark, who didn't believe in ghosts at all, found himself wanting the couple to find something, some kind of proof, to make their visits worthwhile. They were such nice people. But niceness was rarely a guarantee of success in this world.

It was the new year before he saw them again. Mark had stopped expecting a sudden knock on the door, late at night. He had completely given up hope of seeing any ghost on the

stairs himself, with or without feet. His mysterious neighbours on the floor below turned out not to be so mysterious
after all. They were both single men, who worked until the
early hours as taxi drivers. That was why he would hear
them making a noise in the middle of the night, when they
came in from work, but rarely at other times.

One of the main advantages of the flat was that it was
within walking distance of the poly, and some of its halls of
residence. Mark was often invited over by friends who lived
in hall, to visit their cramped but warm rooms. On arriving
at poly, he had put his name down for a place, should
someone drop out of their course and have to leave. Now
though, he was used to fending for himself in the flat, and
liked his independence. It got a bit lonely sometimes,
though. He was often glad to stay out late, talking until the
early hours.

It was on a night like this that Ruth and Ian finally filmed the
ghost. Mark got back to the house just after one in the
morning. Immediately he opened the front door he could
hear something going on upstairs. It was too early for the
taxi drivers to be back, so he guessed it must be Ruth and
Ian. He hurried up the stairs without pressing the timed light
switches. He didn't want to spoil their filming.

Just as he got to the third floor, however, the light came
on in the stairwell leading up to his attic flat. Mark turned
the corner and looked up the stairs. There were Ruth and

Ian, standing in his hallway, the video camera on its tripod beside them. They were jumping up and down, hugging each other, and making whooping noises. Mark coughed, loudly. Ruth and Ian started, then grinned widely when they saw that it was him.

"Mark, we've done it! We've seen the ghost! And we taped it, too!"

Mark hurried up the stairs. Ruth was beaming. She couldn't stop talking.

"You only just missed it. He was as clear as day – an old man, slightly stooped, in an old-fashioned dressing-gown."

"Completely white," Ian added.

"He just appeared at the bottom of the stairs and walked up – only his feet were missing, like he was walking through a bog, rather than up some stairs. He was making this noise. It could have been a moaning, or he might just have been singing to himself – we'll have to listen to it on the tape. It was really spooky. We both thought he was going to walk straight into the camera and us, but just as he reached your front door he seemed to fall. There was this terrible screaming, echoing down the stairwell, then a loud banging, then nothing."

Mark smiled and hugged both of them. He was relieved they'd found their ghost.

"Can I see it then? Your film?"

"Of course," said Ian. "Come on."

They went into the flat. Ian removed the compact video tape from the camera unit, and put it into an adaptor so that it would play in Mark's machine. Then he loaded the tape and pressed the rewind button.

"We only need to go back a little way."

He stopped the tape and pressed 'play'. The stairwell appeared on Mark's portable TV screen, oddly illuminated in a faintly red light. Mark could just make out a gentle breathing sound that must have been Ruth and Ian, sitting beside it. The picture continued in this way for at least two minutes. The three of them sat patiently, eyes glued to the screen, each on the edge of their seat, waiting.

"Any moment now," said Ruth.

There was the sound of someone breathing deeply, followed by a muttered "Oh my . . ." Then the camera jerked, zooming in on the stairway, tracking awkwardly up the stairs until, finally, it pointed at the wall opposite. Then, at last, came the human image. It was Ruth, grinning inanely. She was saying "We did it! We did it!" The tape cut off.

For a few moments, Mark avoided looking at Ruth and Ian. When he eventually turned to them Ruth was crying, making no attempt to hide her disappointment.

"I saw him so clearly," she said. "So clearly."

Ian held her hand.

"Me too. I wish you'd been there, Mark. We both heard . . ."

His voice started to choke and he looked away.

Mark tried to think of words to comfort them.

"At least you saw the ghost. Now you know for sure that

they exist. Obviously they don't show up on film. You've learnt that too."

They didn't answer. Mark got up and switched the TV off. Then he put the kettle on. He remembered the story about the stairs and told it to them.

"You see, that helps to confirm what you and the others saw!"

Ian shook his head.

"But you don't believe it, do you, Mark? You were right all along: ghosts, the supernatural – it's all in the imagination. People see what they want to see. Ruth and I knew exactly what we were looking for and we saw it. Only we'd brought along a camera to verify our findings and it didn't. We wanted proof. In a way, we got it."

Mark poured boiling water on to the coffee granules. He could hardly argue. He'd been proved correct. But he didn't feel good about it.

Ruth wiped her eyes.

"I wouldn't have believed myself capable of that kind of . . . self-deception. Still, our aim wasn't to find ghosts, really. It was to find the truth."

She turned to Ian.

"We can still use what happened to us, can't we?"

Ian nodded. They drank their coffee without speaking. When they'd finished Ian picked up the video camera and Ruth the blanket. Ian spoke calmly.

"We won't be back, I'm afraid. But we'll probably write this misadventure up for *Paranormal Bulletin*. We'll send you a copy when it comes out."

"I'd like that."

Mark kissed Ruth on the cheek and shook Ian's hand.

"Don't see us out," Ian said. "We know the way."

Mark switched on the light in the stairwell for them and they left, walking out of his life as quietly as they had walked into it. He went to bed, but couldn't sleep. He shouldn't have drunk that coffee. He thought about Ruth and Ian – their bitter disappointment. It was possible, he considered, that they *had* seen a ghost. His explanation could be the right one – ghosts existed, but didn't show up on film. Some people could see them, others couldn't. There were so many stories about the paranormal that there must be something in it, even if Mark was too earthbound to see ghosts himself. He would write to Ruth and Ian, he thought, and tell them they might be wrong.

The next day was a Sunday. Mark tried to write his letter to Ruth and Ian, but the words wouldn't come out right. He had a difficult essay due in the next day, so he started on that instead. By three o'clock, his essay was in full swing – another hour and he'd have cracked it. He decided to tape that afternoon's televised football match, and watch it when he'd finished. It was then he realised Ruth and Ian had left their compact tape, with its adaptor, in his video machine.

He ejected it, and put in a blank tape for the football. He'd have to write to them now. Mark wondered whether they'd want him to entrust the tape to the ordinary post.

True, there was nothing to see, but in a way it was still valuable evidence. Maybe they'd want him to use some fancy messenger service. He'd ring tomorrow.

He got to a phone booth at one the next day. He dialled the number that Ruth had scribbled down for him. He had to wait a long time for it to answer. A queue of students formed outside the booth.

"University College."

"Oh, hello. I'd like to speak to Ruth or Ian, please."

The voice at the other end sounded more amused than annoyed.

"I'm afraid you'll have to be a little more specific than that."

In a panic, Mark realised he didn't know either of their surnames. He tried to remember the name of their department.

"They're in . . . I think it's the Department for Paranormal Investigations."

"We have no department of that name."

"Well, something like that. I know the word 'paranormal' is in it."

"I'm afraid you have the wrong university, sir. Try California."

She hung up.

Mark cursed and tried to think.

"Have you finished?"

Reluctantly, he gave up his place at the phone. Over lunch, he tried to work out how to get in touch with them. He could hardly post the tape to people whose surname he didn't know in a department that didn't exist. But it did exist. They'd told him about it. And about their renowned professor who put them on to the story in the first place.

But why had he been told that the department didn't exist? Unless it had another, less controversial name. That must be it, thought Mark. The university would probably be embarrassed to admit to a "Paranormal Investigations" department. They'd have *The Sun* on to them for stories every other day. It would be called something else. All he had to do was track down the professor they'd mentioned. What was his name? Blenkinsop? No, but close. He tried to hear the sound of the word when Ruth had said it. Jenkins . . . Yes, Jenkinson. He'd got it. Once more, Mark queued for the phone.

"University College."

"Professor Jenkinson, please."

"Would that be Jenkinson, Law, or Jenkinson, Psychology?"

"Psychology."

He remembered Ruth and Ian did their undergraduate degrees in Psychology.

"Hello?"

A deep voice answered without a phone ringing first.

"Professor? You may have heard of me. My name's Mark Sullivan. Two of your investigators have been doing some filming at my flat."

"Two of my what?"

The man sounded irritated.

"Ruth and Ian. I don't know their surnames, but they told me about you and the Paranormal Investigations Department."

This time the man sounded angry.

"No such department exists."

"Oh."

"I think somebody's been taking you for a ride."

"Oh."

Mark felt a hollow sensation in his stomach, like he'd been punched. He didn't understand. What possible reason could they have to con him like that? He was about to put the phone down when the professor spoke again.

"They called themselves Ruth and Ian, you say?"

"Yes. They said that you, or someone called Professor Jenkinson, ran this department. They were trying to get proof that ghosts existed."

"Please go on."

The pips went. Mark put in another fifty pence. He found himself telling this stranger his story. When he'd finished, the professor said, "And you still have the videotape?"

"Yes."

The professor paused.

"I think I'd better come and get it."

"What? Why?"

"I'm going to set off now. I should be with you by early evening. Can you make sure you're in?"

"Yes, but I don't . . ."

"I'll explain in person when I see you."

Mark put the phone down. It was only when he got home that he realised he hadn't given the professor his address.

Mark heard the creaking sound of feet on the stairs at five to six. The professor was quite an old man, but an imposing one. He was almost as tall as Ian, but with a lot more hair, so curly that it seemed in danger of getting hopelessly tangled.

"Have you got the tape?"

Mark got it out.

"Would you like to watch it?"

The professor nodded. Mark put it into the machine.

"It just needs rewinding a bit."

The image of the stairwell appeared again. While they waited for something to happen, Mark asked the professor questions.

"Where *are* Ruth and Ian? *Who* are they? Were they really lying to me?"

The professor shook his head.

"Later."

The camera jerked. Once more, Mark heard Ruth's exclamation, followed the camera up the stairs, saw the brief image of Ruth's pretty face grinning. Then it was over. The professor ejected the tape from the machine and put it into his pocket.

"Thank you."

He got up to go.

"Is that it? No explanation?"

"I think you would rather I didn't tell you."

The professor was avoiding Mark's eyes.

"I *want* to know."

The professor opened the door and looked down the stairwell.

"I'll tell you briefly, if you insist. Ruth and Ian were two of my best students . . ."

"*Were?* You mean they don't work for you any more?"

The professor shook his head and stared at the floor.

"Please don't interrupt. This is difficult for me. I put them on this case, one of our most promising, and they visited this house four times in all."

"Yes, I know. I saw them. The last time was two days ago!"

Mark stopped. Suddenly, he felt a sense of impending tragedy. The professor continued.

"After the fourth visit, they rang me. They told me they had seen something which could make the history books if it showed up on the film. They were very excited."

"But . . ."

The professor carried on, ignoring Mark's interruption.

"What they had seen agreed with three earlier reports. I had traced the origins of the story myself, without telling Ruth and Ian, so that they couldn't be influenced by it. In the 1920s, an old man lived in this room, when the place was a boarding house. One night, as he was coming up from the bathroom, the banister rail gave way. He fell from the top of the stairs to the landing below, breaking his neck."

"Did you tell them this on the phone?"

The professor sighed.

"Yes. We were all getting worked up about it. They agreed to come straight to my house in Ealing. We were going to look at the tape together."

He paused.

"I waited up for them all night. They didn't arrive."

"Why? What happened?"

"There was a pile-up on the motorway, just before Watford Gap. Black ice. The police said that they must have died almost instantly."

"No!"

Mark felt numb, the way you do before grief begins to sink in. The professor finished his story.

"Naturally, I assumed that the tape perished with them. I'm afraid I took what happened to them as a kind of message to me, personally. I decided to close the paranormal investigations department and go back to plain psychology."

Mark tried to give the strange man a sympathetic look.

"I see."

For the first time since he'd arrived, the professor looked Mark in the eye.

"*Do you?*"

He turned abruptly and walked down the stairs in the dark.

"Wait!"

Mark switched on the light.

"Ruth and Ian were my friends. I'd like to go to their funerals, if I can. Do you know the arrangements?"

The professor stared up at him from the landing. His gaze was chilling, but he spoke gently.

"That won't be possible, I'm afraid. Ruth and Ian died five years ago."

They stood looking at each other in silence. Then the light clicked off and Mark heard the professor walk away into the night.

THE CRACKED SMILE

Anthony Masters

 enny had told him never to go into the attic, and so far he hadn't. She had always been adamant, but the reasons varied. Sometimes the place was "filthy" or "too much of a muddle"; other times there were "rats" or "mice" or "the door was stuck". So in the end, over the years, he had given up asking. Ian's curiosity had never been that high anyway, for he had assumed that his aunt was probably right and that there was only a dirty muddle up there, with the odd rat or mouse thrown in.

But on this wet Sunday, with his great friend Freddy away on an enforced outing and Jenny busy with an old folks' tea, Ian's curiosity suddenly became too much for him. He *had* to go up there. Now.

They lived in an old Victorian house on the outskirts of town, near a council estate and a factory that manufactured cast iron bearings. Once their house had been part of a wealthy farm and mansion, but now that had all gone and Jenny's house reared up out of the flat landscape, looking old and battered and sour.

Jenny was the only relation Ian had; she was his mother's unmarried older sister, in her fifties now, with a sharp and domineering outer shell and a soft, loving interior. By day she was secretary to the Managing Director of the factory, and for the rest of the time she cared for Ian and did good works for the aged.

Ian's father had left home when he was a baby and his mother and older sister had been killed soon after in a road accident that Jenny never talked about, despite his questions.

"It was a tragic affair," she had told him. "Something I can't bear to talk about. Maybe I'll tell you one day, but not now, Ian. Not now."

He had accepted that it was all too painful for her and had not questioned her for some years; he had not really felt the need. He could remember nothing about his early childhood except being in another house – somewhere small – in the centre of town, sitting in a playpen surrounded by broken, battered dolls. His aunt had at least found herself able to explain that.

"You have to realise you were all very poor, living in that damp cottage. While *he* was out, she had to do anything she could lay her hands on to make money. That was why she started repairing broken dolls – called it a Dolls' Hospital – she was that desperate."

Jenny only ever referred to Ian's father as "him", and refused to talk about him. So over the years, Ian gathered that he only aroused in her feelings of deep hatred.

The attic was approached by a pull-down ladder and a small door that was locked. But Ian knew Jenny kept all her spare keys at the back of the enormous stone larder, and while she was out he found the key he needed after ten minutes of turning each one in the keyhole. At last the door swung silently open and a musty smell immediately hit his nostrils. Using a torch he searched for a light switch, but when he found it, it didn't work so he had to rely on his wide but not very powerful beam.

She was right. The attic was certainly a dusty muddle, but nothing scuttled or ran beneath his feet so he continued to flash the beam around, at first erratically and then more systematically. A dull disappointment crept over him as he realised there was nothing out of the ordinary. He could hear the rain beating down on the roof, and through a grubby skylight could see the overcast, pitted sky outside. He could imagine the leaden rain falling on the council estate and factory, and his sense of disappointment made him feel as miserable inside as the landscape looked outside.

Ian continued his slow inventory of the attic: old furniture, mattresses, a broken table, piles of magazines, books, discarded clothes, a collapsed ironing board, a glass container of stuffed birds, part of a table tennis table, scattered boxes – and in the corner a pile of old, battered, broken dolls. He moved over to them without interest until his beam picked out a single doll, sitting slumped on a tiny chair. A sense of shock filled him suddenly, making his mouth go dry and filling him with an uneasy tingling sensation. But why? There seemed no reason. The doll's face was covered in a mask of dust and Ian rubbed at it tentatively. The result was horrific. One eye remained, the other was a dark socket. The cheeks were scaled and stained, the nose smashed, an ear hung loose and there was a hole in one cheek. But far, far worse were the lips that should have been a pouting bow but instead seemed to be set in a cracked and twisted smile.

Suddenly Ian felt dizzy, and he sat down quickly on an old leather sofa that smelt of decay. Almost immediately his eyelids became incredibly heavy and he felt a lurching sensation as if he were slipping into a void. There was a roaring in his ears and he closed his eyes. When he forced them open again he saw that the room was moving about him, suffused in shadow and then sharply distorted. The roaring sound continued, but above it he heard the screaming of brakes as his eyes closed for a second time. Instinctively he reopened them and saw that he was lying on his side facing the doll with the cracked smile. He whimpered as the smile seemed to widen, and then cried out in terror as tinny laughter whined from her plastic insides. The laughter continued like a cheap music box and then ground to a slow-motion halt. The heaviness lifted and Ian stumbled to his feet and ran to the door of the attic. For a moment he rattled at it desperately but the handle wouldn't move. Suddenly it turned and he wrenched the door open and climbed down the ladder as fast as he could. When he reached the bottom, he was shaking so much that he could hardly stand. The rain seemed to increase in intensity outside and only gradually did his strength return.

The detention room was full of the usual crowd, and Mrs Small was in charge. She would be, thought Ian; she always seemed to enjoy the gloom-charged atmosphere and the resentful scratching of pens and biros. He had gone to bed early the previous night, dazed by his experience, and had slipped into a deep, dreamless sleep. When he woke the attic episode seemed confused and unreal. Yet, throughout the day, he had felt his concentration slipping and at lunchtime, agreeing to play football with Freddy too near the school building, he had broken a window – which had landed him in detention.

He sat and wrote and looked out of the window. It was almost Christmas and a covering of snow a few days before had turned to thick, black slush. It was dark and wet and he wished that Freddy was with him. They had been friends since primary school, and now that they were in their first year at the comprehensive their friendship remained as firm as ever.

"All right – you can go," Mrs Small said eventually. "And no noise."

No one listened as they charged out, heading home for tea and chips and telly. But Ian's bus was not due for another half hour and he sauntered across the playground and down the dark High Street to the bus stop. Glancing at his watch, he saw he still had another twenty minutes before the bus came, so he wandered down a shabby side street, then turned into another smaller street which was even more run-down than the last. He had never been here before, he realised, and looked about with some curiosity. Most of the shops were empty, a small chapel bore a sign saying "Have You Heard the Good News?" and a little weather-boarded cottage, obviously some hundreds of years old, leaned crazily over the pavement. The glass in the windows was broken, the boarding rotting away, and some of the slates on the roof had fallen to the pavement. A small sign over the door, its paint so faded that he could only just make out the words, read "Dolls' Hospital".

Shock waves coursed through Ian. Broken dolls again? Just a coincidence – it *must* be. Down the side of the shop was a little alley, covered in mounds of litter. Slowly, cautiously, he began to walk down it.

"Oi!"

It was Freddy, his blond hair shining in the light of the street lamp, staring at him from behind an old rain barrel. Ian was startled to see him, thinking that he had gone home ages ago.

"What are you up to?" Ian asked suspiciously.

"There's lead on a roof down in this yard."

"So?"

"You can sell lead."

"Can you? Isn't it against the law?"

Freddy ignored him. "Want to take a look?"

Ian glanced at his watch; he still had quarter of an hour before the bus went. Why not?

Freddy led the way through the debris to a sad little moonlit yard, full of dilapidated sheds and tumbling buildings.

"Up there." He pointed.

He was right, thought Ian gloomily, there *was* some lead still in place. Trust Freddy to find it. Then he heard something and whipped round.

"What was that?"

"Eh?"

"There's someone up there."

"Where?" Freddy was still looking at the lead on the roof and trying to estimate how much it would fetch. If there was one subject he was good at it was Maths, and he gave himself plenty of practice.

"In the house."

"Dosser?" He turned round, his fair skin grubby, looking older and harder than his years. "Let's go and surprise him."

"It wasn't like that."

"What *was* it like then?" He was getting bored.

"More like crying. I'm going to take a look!"

"O.K."

For once, Ian had put himself in the position of leader,

and rather hesitantly he walked over to the broken-in back door of the cottage and pushed his way through. Once inside the tiny kitchen, the boys paused, almost overcome by the smell of damp and mould.

"Wow!" said Freddy. "What a tip."

Then Ian heard the sound again, and at the same time felt an extraordinarily overpowering sense of familiarity. He began to shiver, with a chill that started somewhere deep inside him. "Didn't you hear it?"

"No."

"Came from upstairs – someone crying."

Freddy went to have a look. "Better be careful – the wood's rotten."

"You scared?" asked Ian.

"No."

"Let's go up there."

"All I'm saying is . . ." began Freddy.

"The wood's rotten. Yes, I can see it is." Without any further comment, feeling quite normal again, Ian began to climb the stairs, Freddy following rather more cautiously.

The stairs held, despite ominous creaking, and they eventually found themselves on a landing. Obviously someone had been up there, for cans, food wrappings and a couple of bottles lay on the floor.

Ian nudged open one of the doors, but there was nothing inside except piles of rubbish and rubble where part of the roof had collapsed. Then he moved across the landing, pushed open another door and saw her standing by the window.

She was dressed in a pair of old corduroy trousers and a sweater, tears running down her cheeks, her hands clenched into white fists. There was something slightly dated about her clothes, and the sobbing increased as Ian watched from the threshold. Beside her stood a girl of about ten, clutching a doll. That seems odd, thought Ian. Surely she's a bit old for dolls now? She was even more insubstantial than the woman. Around them were vague outlines of benches and tables, and on every surface the grey shapes of dozens of different dolls of all sizes. Most of them looked battered or broken. Ian gasped and his whole body seemed to shake. It was suddenly terribly cold again and he felt freezing inside. Then the woman and the girl bent down. The little girl sat on something and dimly he could see that it was a suitcase. The woman fastened it and they both stood up slowly. Then they walked straight through him.

"Go *on*!"

"Don't push."

"Don't you stand there then."

"Shut up!" Ian wheeled round on the surprised Freddy. "Just shut up. Didn't you see them?"

"Who?"

"The woman, the little girl, the broken dolls –"

"You're seeing things," scoffed Freddy.

"I'm not. They were there."

"They're not there now," Freddy pointed out. "And never were," he added.

"They were," insisted Ian belligerently.

"Look at the dust!" Freddy's voice was impatient now.

He was right. The whole of the floor was covered in thick dust and there wasn't a mark anywhere. Ian felt the chill stealing over him for the third time. Then the words Dolls' Hospital glanced into his mind and a feeling of nausea overcame him. Desperately he tried to resist the thought of what it all meant.

As he walked cautiously across the room, leaving a trail of footprints, he suddenly recoiled and cried out.

"What's up now?" snapped Freddy.

"Something touched me."

"You trying to wind me up by any chance?" Freddy asked icily. "If so, I can tell you – you're not succeeding." There was an uneasy silence.

"You'll miss the bus," said Freddy at last, not knowing how to handle the situation and trying to bring the conversation down to earth again.

"Bus?"

"Yes – big red thing. Four wheels or is it six? Has a driver. Goes on a road. A road's usually black with white lines." He would have continued had Ian not yelled at him to shut up.

"Aren't you coming?" asked Ian hurriedly.

134

"Thought I'd stay around."

"You're going to nick that lead, aren't you?"

"Not now I'm not," said Freddy evasively.

"Yeah?" But Ian didn't have time to stop. He pushed past him and ran down the rickety steps to the alley and then to the street outside. He had a few seconds. He knew he had to catch the bus or Jenny would be furious. He had managed to ring her from school and she had been bad enough over the detention, and he had promised faithfully he would catch the six o'clock bus. Freddy's mother didn't worry so much and she was often out when he got back anyway, so he had to get his own tea.

As he ran, Ian began to feel faint and the shops and houses in the side street seemed to blur. When he turned into the High Street he felt even worse: his head was spinning so much that he had difficulty in keeping his balance and knowing where he was going. Several times he bumped into people, but the odd thing was that he could hardly feel any impact at all. Everything – everyone – seemed out of proportion and the spinning feeling was replaced by a strange surging motion. A swirling mist made the shops look different. Then he saw that they *were* different.

The supermarket didn't seem to be there; instead there was a grocer. A cinema called "The Roxy" occupied the site where the furnishers' had been and petrol pumps fronted what had been a car showroom. He began to notice other changes: an ironmonger's had replaced a hair salon, there was a shoe repair shop instead of a Wimpy, and wasn't that a butcher instead of . . .? He didn't have time to think as the number nineteen bus rumbled down the road. Even the bus was different – a single- instead of a double-decker, with a strange look to it. The mist was hanging about in patches and the people around him seemed almost transparent.

When the bus drew up he was surprised to find that the driver didn't take the fare and there was a conductor instead. Hadn't Jenny told him that conductors had been replaced ages ago? What on earth was going on?

Ian boarded the bus. It was empty except for two passengers near the front. He showed his bus pass to the conductor, who hardly seemed to glance at it but stayed on the back step, watching the street with its shadowy shapes, seemingly intent on anything but the interior. It was weird, thought Ian – the bus was usually quite crowded. Where was everybody? Then he noticed that it was no longer dark outside.

No longer dark? This was ridiculous. Crazy. He glanced at his watch. It was twenty past five on a December evening and yet the mist was parting to reveal morning light. He was sure of it. He must ask someone. Who was up at the front? Ian peered ahead, but despite the hard light outside the interior of the bus was dim, as if all the mist had seeped in. Yes, there were two passengers – one quite small. Maybe a child. He would have to go and investigate.

Glancing at the conductor, he rose from his seat and

walked down the aisle towards the driver and the hunched passengers. When he got there, he recognised the girl who had been sitting on the suitcase. Her shape was much stronger than the woman beside her, who seemed to be shifting and swirling, as if she were part of the mist.

"Excuse me."

She had a round face, a snub nose, freckles and long brown hair that fell to her shoulders. She was wearing a print summer dress, with black formal shoes and white socks, and on her lap was a doll. Yes, thought Ian – she's definitely the girl in the room, but now I can see her much more sharply. She looked up at him warily.

"What do you want?" Her voice was very clear. Then she added, "I can't see you properly."

"I'm sorry – I don't understand why it's daylight. When I set out – it was dark."

She stared at him as if he were crazy and glanced nervously over her shoulder at the conductor, who still seemed oblivious to their presence.

"I won't hurt you," Ian reassured her.

She kept darting little glances out of the window and seemed very agitated, but he sensed she was not afraid of him. She was clearly concerned with something else.

"You shouldn't be here. No one comes on this bus except us – the four of us. You'll have to get off."

"Is that your mother?"

"She can't see you. No one else can see you. No one here. You were in our house, weren't you?"

"Yes."

"What are you?" she asked hesitantly. "Some kind of ghost?"

Ian had been about to ask her the same question, but he didn't dare, for the coldness inside him was increasing so much that he could hardly bear the pain.

"Why is it daylight?" he asked. He felt that if at least he knew the answer to that, it would be a beginning.

But all she could do was to shake her head and repeat, "You must get off. It's very dangerous to be riding with us."

The bus speeded up as they emerged into open countryside. And that was funny too, thought Ian. When he usually made the journey from Middleton, the streets sprawled right up to their home but now there were great rolling fields and isolated spinneys of trees with crows wheeling overhead. He could hear them calling over the engine noise and rattling of the bus. Ian couldn't remember any of this. Maybe they were taking a different route. But even so, why on earth were they going at such a speed?

"Look, isn't he driving too fast?" he asked the girl impatiently.

"He's got to," she replied unexpectedly.

"Eh?"

"He's got to," she repeated fiercely.

"But this is a bus. Buses aren't meant to go fast like this."

"There *is* a reason." There was something wrong with her voice now; it sounded distanced and slightly distorted. Of course there must be something wrong with his ears. That must be it – that explained the muzziness. Maybe that was what had made his sense of balance so odd.

"What reason?" he asked.

"My father's trying to get me," she replied.

"*Get* you?"

"Yes, he lost custody yesterday. But he said he's going to take me away – and he's coming down from Birmingham."

There was a short silence. Then Ian asked abruptly, "Where are you going?"

"To my aunt – my Aunt Jenny."

"*Who*?"

"I said – my Aunt Jenny."

Ian felt as if someone had punched him hard in the chest.

"I know he's taking a risk." Her voice, dislocated though it was, seemed quite steady. "I know he's going very fast."

"Who?" Ian's voice shook as his own disorientation increased.

"The driver. He's Mum's friend. Her special friend. It was the only way – we don't have a car. He said he'd bring his bus – there's a "private" sign on it. We've been doing it for a long time."

"But couldn't your father just come to your aunt's and take you?" He could hardly believe what was happening and the cold inside was burning him.

"Oh, no. Auntie Jenny would stand up to him. She's a really strong person."

"Couldn't Auntie Jenny have come to collect you?"

persisted Ian. The more he heard, the more pain he felt. He began to wonder how much longer he could bear it.

"She hasn't got a car either."

"He really is going fast," said Ian as they swerved round a corner.

"Yes, it's like that. Don't be afraid." For the first time there was warmth in her voice.

"Aren't you a bit old for a doll?"

She shrugged. "I've always had her," she said. "I need her more than ever now."

"Who are you?" he asked.

"You *know* who I am."

"I don't –"

"Can't you see? We're like each other, aren't we?"

"Is it *always* like this?" For some reason he couldn't understand, he didn't want to give her a direct reply.

"This is what we do," she said. "We're always on this bus. All four of us."

"But why?"

"My doll," she said, clasping it to her. "She's going to get hurt – and my mum won't be able to repair her."

"Why not?"

"She's going to die, silly! We're all going to die. We keep on dying – every day. It's awful."

"I don't understand," muttered Ian.

"You do. You do really."

"But *why* are you always dying?"

She didn't reply directly. Instead she said, "I'm so

unhappy about Sally – Sally my doll. I can't bear to think of her all smashed up. Maybe that's why we have to keep on riding on the bus – keep on dying all the time. I must know that Sally's safe."

Ian passed a hand across his face and gave a little cry.

"Are you hurting?" she asked.

"Yes."

Suddenly she brightened up. "Maybe you're here for a reason. You're the first person ever. Will you take Sally – and then get off?"

"How can I? The bus is going so fast."

"Oh, that'll be all right."

"How do you know?"

"I just do. Take her. Take Sally."

She tried to pass the doll to him but Ian grasped misty air. "I can't feel anything."

"It's not working," she said, and tears filled her eyes. "It's not fair – she always gets smashed."

Ian wanted to comfort her, but he had to concentrate on keeping his balance on the now wildly swaying bus. The pain was getting worse and he knew he couldn't bear it much longer.

"There must be a reason," she said again.

"For what?"

"For us being able to see each other – for you coming on board – for us to be able to speak. You and Mum don't seem able to reach each other at all!"

"Maybe it's the doll." The pain receded for a merciful

141

moment and his mind cleared. "She's in the attic." The thought had come into his head quite suddenly, for no apparent reason.

"What?"

"She's in Jenny's attic."

"*You* live there?"

His voice choked. "Where else can I live? Now you're both gone."

She reached out and he felt the cobwebby touch on his forehead, just as he had done in the room in the cottage.

"We left you with Jenny while we went back to the Dolls' Hospital to fetch the last few things. But we never came back. Sally, though – Sally was smashed. Will you have her repaired?"

"I promise." He thought of the crooked, damaged, horrible smile and looked down at the unblemished, waxy face, staring at it hard.

"What are you doing?" she asked, puzzled.

"Remembering how she was, so she can look like that again." The pain suddenly returned, stabbing at him viciously.

"You've *got* to get off," she said urgently.

"No."

"You *must*. It's dangerous."

"Can I see you again?"

"Of course not."

"Please."

"You *must* get off!" Her voice was fainter and the cold pain was sharper, more probing.

"What's your name?"

"Sophie. Doesn't – didn't Aunt Jenny tell you *anything*?"

"No. She was too upset. There aren't any photographs of you or –"

"Mum?"

"I can't say it."

"Poor you. Poor Jenny." She looked down at Sally. "You'll repair her, won't you?" she repeated. "So she'll be just as she is now. Promise?"

"I promise."

"Now go!"

"I'm staying. Anyway, we haven't come to my stop!" He was determined to hang on – to fight the pain.

"This bus never stops." Her voice sounded even more dislocated. "Go!"

The pain increased until Ian was beaten. Angrily he stumbled up the aisle until he came to the step. The conductor gave him a little shove, but it was more like a breeze on his back. He jumped down on to the ground and the bus pulled away amidst a gigantic cloud of dust. Before it had settled another vehicle roared past; it was a Rover – an old model. Ian caught a fleeting glimpse of the face behind the wheel. The driver's expression was contorted with fury and hatred. He knew he had just seen his father.

Another cloud of dust blew up behind the Rover and enveloped Ian. When it cleared, he saw that the alien open countryside had gone, and in its place stood the estate and the house and the factory on the other side of the river in all their tawdry, tatty glory.

After supper, Ian went straight up to his room and pretended to do his homework. Instead, he lay on his bed and tried to think rationally about the extraordinary events of the last few hours: the cottage, the strange misty shimmering and distortion of the streets, the weird bus journey with his sister and her doll and his mother, the pain, and then the shock of seeing the maniacal rage on the face of his pursuing father. Suddenly, amongst all the confusion, he realised something vitally important. Beyond anything else, beyond all the hurting, beyond even the tenuous link with his mother, he was desperate to see Sophie again. His sister. Curious that he was now older than her. Their roles were reversed and he felt deeply protective towards her. What was going to happen to her? What *had* happened to her? Was she a ghost, or some sort of echo, or simply a manifestation of his own fantasies? He looked up at the posters on his bedroom wall – knights and sorcerers, strange beasts and two-headed women. She wasn't like any of those. Sophie wasn't a fantasy.

Later he plunged into a deep and utterly dreamless sleep, and woke refreshed. His mind was completely clear and he knew what he had to do. Today he would see Sophie again, and he would save her from his father.

*   *   *

"Jenny."

"I'm late."

"I want to ask something."

"Ask while I do you an egg."

She was always in a rush in the morning as she had to be at work at eight-thirty.

"Was there ever a single-decker bus on this route?"

"What a funny question." Immediately she was tense.

"Yes, but was there?" he persisted.

"I can't remember," she replied evasively.

"Did they drive fast?" He knew he was persecuting her but he had to know, to be sure that it had all happened. And she knew – she was the only one who could really help him.

"Fast? What a –"

"Funny question. But *did* they drive fast?"

"One did," she said very suddenly, and then she went quiet.

"One?" Ian felt sick. "What do you mean, *one*?"

Jenny looked at him hard. "How did you find out?" she asked brokenly.

Ian shrugged. "It doesn't matter."

"Why do you want to know?" Her eyes seemed to be burning into him.

"I just do. Come *on*, Jenny. You *must* tell me."

"It's not easy for me to explain, especially to you. It was between your parents."

"*And* my sister."

"Yes – well, your father loved them both, you know."

"He loved them – and he did that?" He was incredulous.

"Loved *and* hated, in equal amounts." Her voice was crisp and to the point. "I'm trying to be fair. You know how I feel about him. Anyway, when he lost custody he threatened to take Sophie away. The two of them were at the cottage packing up, and of course Anna – your mother – should have called the police. But she panicked and phoned her boy-friend. He was a bus driver and he brought along an off-duty bus – just took it from the garage. Bill Sampson his name was, and his mate Tim – his usual conductor – came with him. Of course it was all absurd; she'd have been much safer on a regular bus on the route. But she wasn't thinking. None of them were thinking – not even your dad. Peter came to the cottage and found she'd gone and a neighbour told him she'd seen them getting on a bus. He followed, the bus was going at full speed, he tried to overtake –" Her voice shook and broke. "I should have told you all this years ago –"

"No."

"It's the pain."

"I felt that," he said reassuringly. "It was very big. Were they *all* killed?" he went on.

"Your father wasn't. You know he's still alive – some-where."

"Was he – did he go to prison?"

"No. He was prosecuted for dangerous driving, that's all. You can imagine how what he did broke him."

"Yes –"

"Is there anything else?" she asked gently.

146

Suddenly he felt compelled to tell her. "I've been up in the attic."

She stared at him in silence.

"Are you angry?"

"No." Her voice was very low.

"Those dolls –"

"They were the ones your mother was repairing. In all the confusion after the accident they were never reclaimed."

"And the one in the chair? The one with the smashed face?"

"That was Sophie's special doll. She wouldn't give it up even when she got older. It was given to me. Someone found it –"

"Could it be repaired?"

"Well –"

"Please! I'm sure it would make Sophie very happy."

"Yes," said Jenny slowly. "She could be repaired. Her name's Sally."

Ian had no idea how he got through school, but somehow he did. After lunch he wandered down to the far end of the playing fields so that he could be alone and think, although there was really no need. He knew exactly what he had to do.

He trod softly up the cottage's rickety stairs. Suppose they weren't there? Suppose the cottage didn't – couldn't – weave its magic? Would he ever see Sophie again? It was an unbearable thought.

Then he saw them, very vague and shadowy. He could see nothing else – no dolls, no suitcase, nothing. Just the very wraith of an outline. But surely that was enough. Please God that would be enough.

"Go away." The words were somehow in his mind rather than spoken, and he sensed her touch, gossamer soft on his forehead. It felt more like a kiss than a caress.

"We're going to repair the doll," he whispered. "We're going to repair Sally." Then he began to gabble senselessly, "Don't go on the bus – you'll die. If you –"

"Don't be stupid," the thought voice said. "Of course we're going to die. Thank you for Sally. Now go. You must go away."

"I'm going to save you –" He was beside himself with an illogical rage now. "I must save you."

"We're going," the thought said as her outline shimmered and bleached out like a negative. "You can't save us."

"I'll be on the bus!" he yelled.

"No." And she and his mother faded out completely.

He ran down the stairs as fast as he could, out of the cottage, into the alley and down the side street. Things were more dislocated than ever. He seemed to be running through people, through a lamp-post and then through an old-fashioned telephone box. Then he was in what he took to be the High Street, and yes – there was the single-decker bus. It was just drawing away.

He saw Sophie sitting in the front, just where he had seen her before. This time, though, she was very blurred and he could hardly see his mother at all. They seemed to fade even more as he approached them and he began to panic.

"Sophie!"

She didn't turn.

"Sophie." He sat down next to her and the seat felt like cotton wool.

"You shouldn't be here," she said very faintly.

"I'm going to save you!" he yelled.

She said something else he couldn't hear, her beautiful face transparent.

"I'm going to save you."

"You can't."

"I *can* save you!" he shouted. "Get off the bus with me. We can all jump."

The vehicle was shuddering with speed now. It seemed to be going even faster than yesterday as the townscape vanished and the unfamiliar countryside appeared.

"Come on. Get *up*!"

"No." Her voice was clearer.

"You *must*!"

"You can't change things."

"I can – we can. Take my hand." The icy pain lashed at him and he cried aloud in agony.

"No."

"Please."

"You can't *change* things," she repeated doggedly.

To his horror, Ian could hardly see her now.

"My father's coming," she said. "He comes every day."

"Sophie –"

"We have to keep going."

The interior of the bus, Sophie's body, the conductor behind him, his mother in the distance – all were fading into nothing.

"Sophie. Take my hand!"

Suddenly Ian felt her hand in his, warm and comforting. Then he screamed aloud as it turned to ice in his palm. The last traces of everything around him evaporated into a kind of cold steam, and he found himself standing by the road-side. The road narrowed at the bridge a few metres away from him and he saw the bus trying to slow down. Then he heard the screeching of brakes as another shape appeared – the faint shape of an old-fashioned Rover. He fleetingly glimpsed the hard, set face of his father, consumed by hatred. The screeching of brakes seemed to go on forever, then there was a tremendous impact followed by a deep, painful, appalling silence.

Ian lay on his bed, totally exhausted. He cried for a while, weeping for his dead mother and sister, the tears coming as if they would never stop. Then he rose, went down to the kitchen, took the attic key and climbed back up to the landing. He pulled down the collapsible stairs and started to climb them. At the top he paused, wondering if the pain would come back, but it didn't and he unlocked the door. The moon had risen and a warm light filtered into the jumbled interior through the skylight. A beam seemed to soften the pile of broken dolls and threw its jaundiced light on Sally – the doll with the cracked smile. But this time the smile didn't seem evil – just sad.

Ian picked Sally up and kissed her on her battered lips. They seemed strangely soft, but when he ran his hand over them, they were simply fragmented plastic. He kissed them again and whispered, "Don't worry – you're all right. You're going to be mended. I promise."

As he spoke the words he knew in his heart that it was all over for Sophie. Her eternal bus journey had come to an end.

THE OTHER ROOM

Jill Bennett

hey pressed the 'up' button again and again, but there was no response. The lift had stopped working.

Martin and his mother stared at the closed door in dismay. They didn't have much more to take up but both of them were tired, cold and bad-tempered.

"Never mind, dear," Mrs MacHenry said brightly. "Just be grateful that it's only the third – you could have been heading for the eleventh, you know!" And she gave a merry little laugh.

"Silly cow!" Martin's mother muttered under her breath, in no mood for jokes with her social worker. She picked up a travel bag, a rug and a load of supermarket shopping and turned towards the stairs. Martin followed her. His aching arms only just met around the box of kitchen pots and pans he was carrying. Mrs MacHenry, smiling with determination, brought up the rear.

Well, she thought as she tramped up the concrete staircase,

trying not to notice what was scrawled on the walls, it's a sight better than the hostel. Sharon will soon feel the benefit of a place of her own and Martin will get a chance to breathe a bit. Poor scrap, she could have added, but in her job she saw many children worse off than him. Privacy in a two-bedroomed flat was luxury after all.

She paused at the door of the flat. Martin and his mum were standing in the centre of the living room, their baggage all around them.

"Home sweet home!" Mrs MacHenry's voice was brighter than ever. "Come on, dear – we'll put on the kettle and have a nice cup of tea. Where's the teapot?"

She was gone at last. Sharon Butts sipped the last of her tea and stared at the biscuit crumbs on the melamine worktop. She didn't look old enough to have a boy of Martin's age.

"I'm going to look around." Martin slid off his stool and walked through the rooms. Sharon heard him opening and shutting doors and cupboards.

"Its OK, Mum!" he called. "I've found my room."

"Well, you didn't have far to travel." His mother went to join him, her mood lightening in response to his. She ruffled his hair. "Get your stuff in here, and we'll go and get a pizza tonight."

"Great!"

Martin was sure it was all going to be different now they had a place of their own. Going out with his mum for a pizza must be a sign that a new chapter was beginning.

This was to be his real home. He could just remember living with his gran in her small flat. When she went into hospital he and Sharon had moved into a room above a grocer's shop somewhere. He never knew why they left and went to live with another woman and her two boys. Martin hated it there. It was so cramped and his mum and the woman were always shouting at each other. Then the police came and took the woman off for shoplifting. Martin didn't know what had happened to the boys. He hadn't liked them much. So they went into the hostel. It was all right there, he supposed – there was always someone to chat to and be with when his mum went out, but he hardly ever had her to himself. When they were alone together she was abstracted and rather touchy. He hadn't known where he was with her. But all that was going to change.

Martin didn't know who his father was. He wasn't really bothered. Now and then when boys talked of what they did with their fathers he wished he could do the same, but for the most part he didn't give it a thought.

He had had to leave school in mid-term. The council had given them a home where they could and it meant moving to a new district. He dreaded the idea of starting at the new school. They were halfway through the Christmas term – he'd never fit in. How long had he been at his last school? Martin was beginning to lose track, he had been to so many different ones.

"I'll think about all that tomorrow, when I have to," he

decided as he flung his football boots into the bottom of his new cupboard.

"Mum!" he shouted happily. "You ready yet?"

Sharon tipped her clothes on to her unmade bed and reached for her coat.

"Right then, Mart!" she called back. "Race you down the stairs!"

As Martin walked home from school a week later he remembered the first evening. They were both so hungry they'd wolfed their pizzas and great slabs of Black Forest gâteau. Sharon had laughed a lot and as they planned their new life he'd felt that they were going to be a team at last – two against the world! It's been downhill all the way since then, he thought drearily.

School was as bad as he had feared. Worse, if possible. He didn't know anyone and no one seemed to want to know him. Children who had joined at the start of the term now behaved as if they'd been there for ever. Christmas activities had all been going for some weeks, and although the teachers tried to include him in their concerts or plays he couldn't keep up.

To make matters worse he was given a lot of homework. Most of it looked like double-dutch, especially the maths. If he asked his mum for help she either just laughed or shrugged at him irritably.

"For Pete's sake, Mart! Give us a break!" she said again and again.

"If I knew who Pete was," Martin shouted at her one evening, "I'd ask him!" But that only got him into trouble.

"Thank heavens it's Friday!" Martin scuffed his toecaps over some loose stones, scattering them in front of him. He was taking a short-cut over the patch of ground that stretched under the first floor of the two blocks of flats. Like many others the flats were built on stilts. This created a throughway from one side of the block to the other. Rows of new terraced houses bordered two sides of the central square where the flats stood on a rise. Down the third side, a row of bungalows had been built for elderly people. On the fourth side of the square stood houses that had escaped the heavy bombing of the area during the Second World War.

Martin's feelings of frustration welled up in him and he gave the stones an extra-vicious kick. He didn't even flinch when he heard them clatter against the sides of one or two cars that were parked under the flats. Feeling better, he did it again.

"'Ere! Who's doing that?"

As he came out from the underpass, Martin halted.

"You got all that grit in my bag and on my hands! It didn't half hurt!" An old woman had dropped her shopping and was on her hands and knees picking it up. "Might have known it was a kid."

Martin stared at her.

"Well, cat got your tongue?" She sat back on her heels and gently rubbed the back of one hand with the other.

Martin stumbled forward. Awkwardly, he began to pick

up the scattered groceries and put them in the shopping bag lying on the ground. He was blushing furiously, his face nearly as red as his hair. He felt that somehow he must have been responsible for the broken handle on the bag, and the cracked eggs he could see leaking on to a bag of tomatoes. She looked so old and fat and he didn't know what to say.

"'Ere," she said again, "give us a hand up! It's cold down 'ere."

Martin took one of her hands in its knitted glove and, putting his other hand under her elbow, gave a heave. To his relief it brought her to her feet. She was as round as a barrel but not much taller than he was when she was standing upright.

He handed her the broken bag of groceries and she clutched them to her chest in an ungainly way.

"You don't say a lot," she remarked, peering at him under a ragged grey fringe. "D'you live here?"

"Hang on—" Martin made a dive for a tin of rice pudding that lurched out of the lopsided bag. He retrieved it. "Give it here," he added, putting the tin in his coat pocket and fishing out other items that were threatening to overflow.

"I'll carry these for you," he told her, glad to be able to do something that made him feel better.

"Over 'ere then." The old woman stumped off over the grass to the bungalows. Martin followed her.

At the front gate she turned to face him. "Put them things on the step," she ordered, fishing out her key. "And if anyone asks you, it's Mrs Collins you've been talking to."

She paused and gave him another of her looks from under her fringe. "You got a name?"

"Um, Martin," he said, embarrassed.

Mrs Collins grunted and turned back to her front door.

Martin let himself into the flat and dropped his school bag on the sitting room floor. He went straight into the kitchen and put the kettle on. With one movement he opened the bread bin and took out some slices of bread. He spread them with marge from the fridge and layered on some chocolate spread. As the kettle boiled he scooped it all on to a plate and slid a teabag into a mug. I could do this in the dark, he thought, as he poured the hot water on to the teabag and added milk.

He turned on the TV and put the first slice of bread and spread into his mouth. He continued to watch the children's programmes until he had finished eating, with only half his mind on what he was seeing. The rest of it was still wrestling with the difficulties of his school day.

Feeling restless, he got up and wandered over to the window. The winter dusk was already deepening into night. Martin watched the mist gathering across the patch of grass and masking the ends of the streets. He wished his mother were there. She wouldn't be back for ages. She had got a job at a supermarket a bus ride away and it would be gone six o'clock before she got home.

He picked up his school bag and dragged it on to the table

that stood against the wall. This was the outside wall. It had no windows in it and was covered in a dull beige wallpaper. Sharon had stuck a poster of a pop group on it, but one edge was already peeling off. Martin found it depressing. Also, he got an odd feeling when he thought that there was nothing on the other side of the wall. Only space. And right now, dark space.

He left his books in the bag and sat down. Putting both elbows on the table he stared ahead, straight at the wall.

The television was wittering on behind his back, but he didn't hear it. He felt tired and very empty. The beige wall seemed to waver under his stare. His mind drew shadows on the wall which turned into shapes, and he let himself go with them. It gave him a hazy sensation that was a little bit like swimming.

In his half-aware state he didn't notice the change in the beige wall at first. When he did, it came as a shock.

The wall had disappeared. In its place was another room. True, it was all a bit hazy, as if it had a net curtain in front of it, but it was there.

Martin blinked hard, but the room didn't go away. It was obviously a room because he could see its three walls. Only the fourth wall – the beige wall – was missing. His head spun. He looked away and back again. It was still there.

He leaned forwards against the edge of the table and peered at it.

The room was lit by a standard lamp and the glow from a gas fire. The lampshade was a sort of pink colour, making the room look warm and cosy. It was hard to make out the rest of the furniture with the net curtain effect in between, but Martin thought that the ceilings sloped a little as if it was an attic room. He loved attics. They had so many funny shapes in them, and unexpected nooks and crannies. Was there someone in the room? He couldn't tell.

"It's like a freezer out there!" The front door of the flat slammed shut and made him jump, and the strange room immediately disappeared. His mother was stamping her feet on the carpet. "Its not much better in here. Martin, didn't you turn the heating on, for goodness' sake?"

Martin started guiltily, confused for a moment. Was his mother home early or had he been staring at the wall for longer than he knew? He realized he was feeling very cold.

Sharon strode over to feel a radiator. "That's hot," she said.

"I don't have to turn on anything," Martin protested. "It's on all the time here."

"Well, I don't think much of it."

Martin's heart sank. His mum was obviously in a bad mood. Perhaps it had been a long wait at the bus stop. It didn't take much to rub her up the wrong way.

"I got your supper on the way home. "Sharon put a bundle of fish and chips on to the table in front of him. The warm smell of fish and oil wafted up. Martin felt hungry. He opened the paper and pulled out a chip.

161

"Get a plate, you lazy tyke!" Sharon still hadn't taken her coat off and was looking at him uncertainly.

"Where's yours?" Martin had fetched a plate and a knife and fork from the kitchen. He was balancing the bottle of sauce on top.

"Mart," his mother began to reach for her scarf, "I'm going out. I said I'd meet some people in the Queen's Arms after work."

"What people?" Martin demanded.

"Just people. I don't have to answer to you." Sharon's voice rose truculently. "And watch what you're doing with that sauce!"

"What are you waiting for then?" Martin slammed the plate and sauce bottle down on the table and turned his back on his mother.

He heard the front door open. "'Bye, Mart! Don't watch the telly too late." Then he heard the door shut and her footsteps walking quickly away.

Martin tipped the fish and chips on to the plate in a heap. He opened the sauce bottle and jabbed it viciously to get the sauce out. It fell out in a dollop, smothering the chips. He tried to scoop some back with a chip but it landed in the bottle and he swore. Pushing it away he seized the plate and went to watch television.

He ate his dinner with his fingers. His mum wasn't there, so why should he bother? he asked himself. It tasted good like that anyway. He watched a TV police series half-heartedly, wiping up the last of his sauce with his fingers,

then took his empty plate to the kitchen where he left it in
the sink, and wandered aimlessly back into the sitting room.
He was just about to spread out on the sofa and put his feet
on one of the arms, a position that he knew infuriated
Sharon, when he felt a draught of cool air brush his cheek.
He turned round towards the beige wall – the other room
was back.

Martin felt afraid. He ducked down behind the back of the
sofa and glared at the television with all his might. But he
had to raise his head and look to see if the room was still
there, on the other side of the beige wall.

It was.

There was something so attractive about it. He was drawn
to it like a magnet. His heart thumped hard as he got up and
went towards it. He sat in his chair and faced it full on.

Someone was in the room. There was a figure sitting
on an armchair by the gas fire. Martin could see it was a
woman. A child was sitting at her feet and another one
curled up on a cushion. He squinted with the effort of
trying to see more. All at once the woman rose quickly
and the two children scrambled to their feet and the light
went out. For a second Martin was staring at total
blackness and then the beige wall seemed to hit him in
the face.

It was gone.

The draught of cool air, too, was shut off as if someone
had closed a window. Slowly he returned to the sofa, and
after a moment realised that the police story had finished

and the weather forecast was on. He had missed the news as well, but it had seemed that he had only been watching the room for a minute at the most.

The key rattled in the lock and his mother came in.

She took his silence for reproach and, flinging her coat on a chair, plumped down beside him on the sofa and gave him a little push.

"Come on," she said. "Give us a smile!"

Martin managed a weak one. He was very glad that she had come in just then, for he was still feeling shaken.

"You're pale," she observed, taking a good look at him. "Even for you." Martin's white skin never had much colour. "Got a pain?"

"Mum," Martin began. He stopped, trying to find the right words to tell Sharon what he had seen without it sounding barmy. His mother broke in.

"Now don't you start. It's bin a rotten day. You don't grudge your mum a bit of fun, Mart, do you, eh?" And she gave his hair a playful tug.

Martin didn't know how to answer his mother when she was like this. It was good to be sitting on the sofa side by side, to have her sounding happy and playful. Sometimes she didn't seem like a mum. Martin wished she would play with him more often, but it usually only happened when they'd had a row.

He decided to tell her about the room another time.

They sat together a bit longer till Sharon shooed him off to bed.

Well, he thought, it's the weekend tomorrow. Perhaps we'll do something nice.

As he got into bed, however, he didn't think they would. On Saturdays Sharon got up late, went shopping, and either spent hours watching TV or else had a visitor – usually Charlie, who wasn't interested in doing anything much except drinking beer and watching football. Martin didn't mind that – he liked football. But then his mum and Charlie went out, giving him money for a takeaway. On Sundays Sharon got up even later and never seemed to be in a good enough humour to go anywhere or do anything.

Martin sighed and buried his head in his comic. He always read till he fell asleep.

Charlie downed the last of his beer at about seven o'clock and stretched. Saturday had followed its usual pattern. "Right, Sharon girl!" he said. "Get your coat on."

"Charlie," Sharon didn't get up right away, "how about us getting a video tonight?" She glanced at Martin anxiously. "We've bin out a lot this week."

"You do it if you like, girl!" Charlie was putting on his jacket. "I'm going down the pub. See you later then?"

Sharon hesitated. Then she gave in. Charlie grinned as he pulled a ten pound note out of his pocket and held it out to Martin.

"Get yourself something really nice, Mart."

"Don't call me that!" Martin exploded.

"Martin!" Sharon glared at him, but Charlie shrugged.

Martin kicked at the sofa legs miserably. He didn't mind his mum calling him Mart sometimes, but that was it. They were begining to call him Change at his school. Exchange and Mart was too long. Martin supposed it was better than Sunset or Carrots.

What's the point of having a name, he thought glumly, if nobody calls you it?

"Come on, old son," Charlie said. "We'll walk you to the video shop. Can't say fairer than that, can we?"

Martin put his coat on and they clattered down the stairs into the wintery night.

He chose a video with as many monsters on the cover as possible. The Take Away Kebab was nearby in the parade of shops on the old side of the square. Feeling rich with Charlie's money Martin chose chicken, a can of cola, and two portions of chips. He was nearing the door with the warm packet under his arm when he heard a voice.

"Ere, um-Martin!"

Mrs Collins was sitting at one of the tables, tucking into a steak and kidney pie.

Martin grinned at her in surprise.

"Sit down," said Mrs Collins. "Be my guest."

"Go on," she added, seeing him hesitate, "I won't bite you."

Martin did so. His mother always told him to go straight home. Why should he? She wasn't around.

"Well," said Mrs Collins with her mouth full, "get stuck in then."

They ate together in silence for a bit. Martin grew warm with the food and the company. He ate ravenously.

"That'll make your hair curl!" Mrs Collins observed when he finished and pushed the paper to one side. Then she laughed uproariously, for Martin's hair was already very curly. She laughed so heartily that Martin joined in too, although he didn't think it was that funny.

Still chuckling she said, "I'll get us a cuppa – don't get up. Where d'you live, then?" Martin watched fascinated while Mrs Collins spooned four heaped spoonfuls of sugar into her cup. He told her.

"Ah," she said as she stirred the sugar in thoughtfully. "I remember what it was like before they built those flats – and my bungalow if it comes to that."

"Have you lived here long?" Martin plucked up enough courage to ask Mrs Collins a direct question.

"My word, yes," she replied. "Born and bred around here. My dad ran a sweet and tobacconist's shop before the war. Got bombed of course, like nearly everything else."

"Bombed . . ." Martin echoed. There was something so final about that word – bombed. He had seen pictures of bomb devastation – who hadn't – but thinking of it here, where they were sitting, made him feel funny.

"What was it like?" he almost whispered.

"I was a young woman then." Mrs Collins's eyes had a faraway look. "I joined the ATS, the women's army, soon

167

after it began, so I wasn't home much. That's when I met Mr Collins. We were allowed home on leave from time to time. The thing was, we didn't know what we'd still find standing each time we returned. The gasworks was the trouble. For some reason the Jerries made a bee-line for it night after night. They got it in the end."

Martin tried to imagine a shifting, disappearing landscape of houses and rubble. He shivered a little.

"That's a ghost going over your grave, when you shiver like that." She gave him her under-the-fringe look. "You look like a ghost yourself! You'd best be getting home, in the warm."

"What about the houses where our flats are?" Martin wanted to know.

"They were the best," Mrs Collins said. "There was a group of four big houses with lovely gardens. They got too big for some of the owners when coal and that was short, so a couple of them became boarding houses." She saw Martin's raised eyebrows. "Oh you know, they had people lodging there, they let rooms." She got up. "Come on, young man – you can see me home if you want. I like a handsome escort." Martin, still wishing to know more, followed her out.

Leaving Mrs Collins at her gate, Martin ran home. It was one of those dead cold winter nights with no stars. The flat did not welcome him. Empty cans of beer stood on the coffee table, and Charlie's cigarette ends filled the room with their stale smell. With a thrill Martin remembered what had happened the evening before. He had quite forgotten it in the boredom of the day. He looked towards the beige wall and saw it shift and darken. With growing excitement he walked towards the table and sat down. He hadn't even taken off his coat.

The net curtain effect had gone. The room was clear. He took in the details eagerly. The ceiling sloped in two places, with skylights in the slopes. There was some sort of flowery wallpaper and a mantelpiece with a tiled place for a gas fire. The lamp was behind the armchair, shedding its glow on to the lap of the woman who was sitting in it. On the rug in front of the fire two children were sitting playing cards. There was no carpet on the rest of the floor, only some shiny covering. Martin thought it looked cold in contrast with the feeling of warmth around the light.

The boy was about Martin's age and his sister a couple of years younger. The boy had his hair cut very short, while the girl's hair hung in two plaits tied at the ends with bows. The boy was wearing short trousers and knee socks. Martin thought he looked odd.

The children finished their game and the little girl leaned back against her mother's knee. She stroked her hair absently. She was holding a piece of paper in her hand, reading it again and again. It was a letter. Martin could just make out the fact that it had strips of wording cut away. There was almost no letter left.

The woman sighed. Martin jumped. He didn't expect to be able to hear anything. It made him feel unbearably excited and he waited for more, holding his breath.

"I won." The boy spoke.

"You always do," his sister said without much feeling.

What were they playing? thought Martin.

"Mummy?" The little girl turned her head and looked at the letter in her mother's lap. "What did Daddy say?"

Her mother smiled wryly. She held the ruined letter out. "He sends all of us his love," she said. "At least the Germans didn't cut that out."

Then, again with no warning, the family got quickly to their feet and the light went out. A black void hovered for a second in its place and disappeared.

"Don't go!" Martin said aloud as the beige wall closed around him. He felt intensely lonely. He also felt cold.

"What's happening to me?" He looked round his bleak sitting room. When he was looking into the other room he felt such an intense curiosity and a longing to be part of that intimate family circle enclosed by the glow of the standard lamp.

He flung himself down on the sofa in front of the blank television set and tried to think. He tried to imagine himself telling his mother and even Mrs MacHenry about it, but he couldn't.

"There's this room, Mum, that appears on the other side of the sitting room wall." Well, if that bit sounded daft what would the rest sound like?

Anyway, he thought, it's my secret. I want it. He went over the moments again, trying to find a clue to help explain the things he had seen. They all looked old fashioned, that was clear enough, and the mother had mentioned the Germans. Martin made a link.

"It's the Second World War time!" His heart gave a leap. He had seen films and photographs to do with those days and it all fitted in. "I'll go to the school library on Monday," Martin resolved. "Maybe I can find out about that funny letter." But he really wanted to know more about the two children and their mother. He went over it all again many times before he fell asleep. He forgot to watch the video.

Sharon and Martin watched the video together on Sunday afternoon. Martin's eyes kept straying to the beige wall.

"You're getting on my nerves, Martin, staring at nothing like that. What do you expect to see there?" Sharon remarked.

They won't come if she's here, thought Martin, and he found himself wishing Sharon would phone Charlie and go out, but she didn't.

The next day he plundered the school library for Second World War books and studied them when he could. He rushed back from school to see if the room would come to him. It did. Over and over again. His mother came and went as before, sometimes leaving a frozen dinner for him to put in the oven; sometimes bringing in a takeaway, eating it with him and then going out again; sometimes – not often – staying in and watching TV.

Martin began to hate that. Everything was going on in the other room and he wasn't there to see. He had begun to think of them all as "his family". They didn't do anything very exciting, but he just loved to watch, and feel included in their warm family life.

Sometimes the mother mended piles of socks and woollies. She darned them painstakingly, matching the wool carefully. Other times she knitted. This was always khaki wool scarves for the soldiers.

The children teased her about their length when she held them up against them to be measured. They kept close to the gas fire. Sometimes they brought their books – Martin thought some of them were school books. Or they drew pictures or played board games – favourites like draughts and ludo. Martin could hear the radio playing in the background.

The little girl sometimes irritated her brother. Martin quite understood – she could be a nuisance.

At school he began to question everyone he could think of about the war. All his teachers were too young to remember it, but they lent him books and helped him where they could. It got to the point where they began to think he was obsessed by the war, and in a way he was.

The more he learned, the more he could understand the

family's conversation. The ARP, the blackout, the names of
bombers and battleships became familiar. He still hadn't
discovered why that letter on the first real day was so cut
about. They hadn't mentioned it again.

But in the middle of doing something, of speaking even,
they would scramble to their feet and the light would go out.
It was as if they could hear something that he wasn't able to.
Martin couldn't understand it and it left him feeling rejected
and alone.

The second half of the term rolled on, and what had been
difficult to Martin at the start was impossible and uninterest-
ing now. The other children teased him to begin with, making
Churchill's V-sign at him and pretending to be air-raid sirens,
but when they got no response they left him alone.

A week before the end of term, Sharon had gone out after a
supper of fish and chips and Martin was sitting in his place at
the table, engrossed with "his family".

The children had been playing draughts. Shirley (Martin
knew their names by now) had beaten John by a short head
and he pushed the board away in disgust. The black and white
counters scattered over the rug.

"Don't sulk," said Shirley a little smugly.

"I'm not." John turned away and reached for a book. "I let
you win anyway."

"You know you didn't!" Shirley's indignant voice reached
Martin loud and clear.

Was it his imagination or had John's eyes paused briefly and looked into Martin's as he turned? He longed more than ever to play with them. He knew he could beat John any day. They did such lovely things. They built tall card houses with their playing cards. Martin held his breath with them as the houses grew, each layer balanced more and more delicately on the one below.

He also knew that their father was away in the war. They talked about him and wondered how he was. He was in the army, although it wasn't clear where he was.

He grew to recognise the music on the radio when it played dance tunes or songs for the men serving in the war. Shirley and John knew the words and Martin was getting to know them as well. They all sang along together. It was playing dance music now. Their mother got up and held out her arms. "Waltz with me, John," she said.

"Oh, Mother!" John scowled at her.

His mother laughed. "Well, dance with Shirley, then."

"No fear!" Shirley turned her back and John pushed her.

Martin laughed with them. For a split second the children in the other room paused, listening to something, Then, with the usual maddening abruptness, they scrambled to their feet and the lights went out.

The next day Sharon pushed her way through the front door of the flat with her arms full of shopping.

"Whew!" she exclaimed. "That's Christmas for you, Mart! I got my first present today."

"Christmas!" Martin had forgotten about Christmas. He forgot most things.

"Are you living in a different world from the rest of us?" Sharon dumped her bags on to the sofa. "Look, Mart, you've got to pull yourself together. Mr Roper wants to see me about you. What have you been doing at school?"

Martin couldn't think of anything to say.

Sharon felt anxious about him. He was so quiet these days. In one way it suited her that he didn't seem to care if she left him alone any more, but then he didn't care about anything much. He hadn't even said what he wanted for Christmas. She'd asked him once or twice and he'd only said he'd think about it. That wasn't like him. There was something about his pale, wan face that touched her and she went across and put her arms round his shoulders.

"Oh, come on, Mart, let's have a smile!" That had always worked before.

Martin smiled mechanically at her. He was thinking, I think they saw me last night. I think they knew I was there. I wish she'd go.

It was the week before Christmas. Sharon didn't get off work until lunchtime on Christmas Eve, so Martin was given lists of things to buy and do. She wrote everything down and stuffed the lists and money in his pockets to try and make him remember what he had to get. He did his best to do what he was asked. It meant he could be at home with "his family", and he was happy. John had turned and looked at him the last time – he just knew it. The thrill that went through him then was like nothing he had ever felt before. He longed for it again and for Shirley and, above all, their mother to look at him too.

Struggling home with two bags full of tins and food for the Christmas break, he saw a familiar figure just in front of him. Martin broke into a run.

"Mrs Collins!" He panted up beside her.

"'Ere!" she said in surprise. "It's whatsisname."

"Martin," said Martin.

"I got a trolley now," Mrs Collins said proudly. "I gave up on those bags. They was always bursting."

"I remember." Martin grinned. He liked Mrs Collins and he was glad to see her again. She knew all about the Second World War – she'd been in it.

"Put some of your shopping on top of mine," she told him. "There's room, and I'll give you a lift." He did so gratefully, and walked along with her, trying to work out how to ask what he wanted to know.

"Mrs Collins," he began, "when you were in the war did you ever see letters with holes in them?"

"Censored, d'you mean?"

"I don't know, the one I saw had bits cut out all over it."

"Where'd you see that, for heavens' sake?"

"Oh, er . . . in a photo. In a book in the library." He didn't think she'd ask that.

"I remember them letters," she stopped outside her gate and leaned on the trolley. "Dratted things."

"Who sent them?" Martin asked eagerly.

"Well, the boys in the services sent them. But if they held any information that the powers that be thought you shouldn't know, they just cut them out. Sometimes all I got from my Colly was 'Dear Edie' and a lot of 'ands' and 'buts' and then 'your loving husband, Bert'. I could'ov killed the lot of them!"

"Did the Germans do that too?" Martin persisted.

"I suppose they did, same as us."

"No," Martin kept on, "to letters that came to *us*."

Mrs Collins frowned, then she said, "You mean letters from blokes who were prisoners of war? They'd do that right enough."

"He's a prisoner of war," Martin breathed, not realising he was talking out loud.

"What you talking about?" demanded Mrs Collins. "You playing a game or what?" To his great relief she didn't stop for his answer. She was following her own memories.

"This time of year was always worst. Christmas. Worse for the families without their men, and the soldiers, but worst of all for the poor blighters behind the wire."

"What was it like to have Christmas in the war?" Martin could see that Mrs Collins was ready to remember.

"Oh, we did what we could to have a good time. People

saved things through the year for Christmas. Yes," she smiled to herself, "we had some good times. We were all in it together. People seemed to care about what happened to others." She gave a sigh. "You could drop dead today!"

"Did the Germans stop bombing at Christmas?" Martin tried to keep Mrs Collins to the point.

"Not likely!" A shadow crossed her face. "Come to think of it, those big houses up by your flats caught a packet on Christmas Eve. Yes, I remember – I was back on leave that time and we was all in the Queen's Arms' cellar during the raid, keeping the Christmas spirit flowing." She chuckled at the memory. "We heard it fall and knew it was close." She fell silent.

"What happened?" Martin prompted her.

"We went outside after the 'all clear'. What a mess! We could see that the houses were down – there was ever such a large ball of smoke. We all ran up to help if we could. The ARP lot were there first and then the ambulance screamed along. I don't like to think of it, really."

But Martin couldn't let it go. "Did you know anyone there?"

Mrs Collins sighed. "Not really. We knew some by sight but there was a bit of coming and going with the lodgers and that. There was one family who was there longer than most, though. I knew that as my sister gave the lady a hand from time to time. Nice woman." Mrs Collins shook her head sadly.

"The bit I remember most – I'll never forget it – was when

they took a little girl out. She didn't have a scratch on her as far as I could see. Looked just as if she was asleep." She paused. "There was something odd about that bombed house—"

"Was the little girl dead?" Martin broke into her train of thought.

"Of course she was dead." Mrs Collins spoke roughly. "You'd be dead if a few tons of explosive landed on your roof!" She stamped her feet. "Blimey, it's cold! You get along home, boy, and forget all this morbid talk. Have a happy Christmas." And she turned into her gate.

Martin carried his heavy bags home in a trance. Their dad's a prisoner of war, was all he could think. He couldn't wait to see them again, knowing that. Now he really felt like them. As if he were their brother and he had a dad who wrote letters from behind the wire.

As soon as he sat in his chair the other room appeared as if it had been waiting for him. The woman was asleep in the armchair, her face looking pale in the light of the glowing lamp. John and Shirley were doing a puzzle in a comic book, sitting on the floor together, in their usual place. Martin watched their progress happily. At last John finished the puzzle and, with a nudge in Shirley's ribs, he looked straight at Martin and grinned. Shirley looked up, confused for a second, then she too looked out at Martin. She smiled quickly at him and looked away. She must be able to see me too, thought Martin joyfully.

Sharon came in with her arms full of Christmas tree.

The other room vanished promptly.

"Why do you always spoil things?" Martin shouted at her. She stopped with her mouth open in greeting, amazed. Martin, realising too late what he had said, hung his head.

Sharon felt that she was out of her depth with him. There was silence between them, then she said quietly, "It's Christmas Eve tomorrow, Mart. I was only going to ask if you had anyone you wanted to invite over Christmas."

"No thanks, Mum," Martin mumbled.

"Suit yourself." Sharon walked through into the kitchen. "I'm in tonight. Let's hope there's something worth watching."

"Oh, not tonight!" Martin's frustration knew no bounds. His family were about to speak to him – he knew it.

But there was nothing for it. He had to wait.

Before she left for work next morning, Sharon tipped a bundle of decorations on to the floor and said cheerfully, "All yours, Mart. Make the place into a fairy palace. I'm home lunchtime."

With a sinking feeling Martin realised he hadn't even got her a present. Was his family having Christmas too? he wondered. And what about their dad? How was he going to have Christmas behind the wire?

He made a big effort. There was still a lot of Charlie's money left. He would go and get something now. At the parade of local shops he bought a basket of soap and talcum powder done up with a blue ribbon for Sharon and a big packet of small cigars for Charlie. But he thought, I wish I could send them to Dad. Then he remembered he didn't have a dad. They – his family – did.

He felt as if he were only half awake. His other half was making up all the things he was going to talk about that evening. Perhaps . . . perhaps . . . but Martin did not even dare think about it.

When Sharon came in she looked at his halfhearted efforts at decoration in mock dismay. By teatime Charlie found them getting ratty with one another, but the tree was nearly respectable.

"Hello, Charlie!" Martin greeted him with more enthusiasm than he had ever done. Now Charlie was here, perhaps he and Sharon would go out.

"Hello yourself, Mart!" Charlie said, surprised, and put his hand in his coat pocket. "Guess what I've got?" And he waved an envelope about.

"They look like tickets," Sharon made a grab and missed.

"For the panto, girls and boys – *Puss in Boots* at the Town Hall. It's not the West End, but it'll be a laugh. Tonight!"

"That's a lark," Sharon said happily. "Isn't it Martin?"

Martin couldn't speak. No, said his inside voice. No. No. No.

"I – can't go—" He thought desperately for something to say that would convince them he couldn't. "I feel sick." He clutched his stomach.

"Sick, Martin?" Sharon sounded anxious.

Help! thought Martin, I mustn't be so sick they'll stay.

"It's not that bad, really," he went on. "I just feel I might *be* sick. I'd hate to be sick halfway through the show."

"I can't leave you on Christmas Eve," wailed Sharon.

"Here we go!" Charlie began to sound annoyed.

"I'll be fine, Mum. Really." Martin sounded brave and cheerful. "I'll be in the warm, and there's good things on the telly."

Sharon forgot Martin's lack of interest in the telly and weakened.

"All right, love, since Charlie's been kind and got the seats. We'll be back as soon as it's over, won't we, Charlie?"

"Spot on," said Charlie. So they went.

"Now!" Martin flung himself on his familiar chair. There, in the other room, his family were hanging up paper streamers. Their mother held them and Shirley and John were looping them above the fireplace. There were one or two cards on the mantelpiece and a small red candle stood at each end.

"That's pretty." Their mother nodded at them when the streamers were in place. "Get the matches, John. We'll light the candles."

"You light them," she said when he held them out. "Be careful."

Shirley and Martin and their mother watched as John lit the candles. Two little pinpoints of flame added to the warm circle of light. John turned and looked at Martin as if to say, "What d'you think?"

"Lovely!" Martin said aloud. John grinned at him and Shirley looked around in response to the sound of his voice.

"They really can hear me now, I'll be able to join in at last." Martin could hardly believe it.

He saw John and Shirley exchange a look and turn together to their mother. They whispered something in her ear. "Of course," she told them, and she turned too and smiled at him. "Come and join us, Martin," she said, holding out her hands.

Happiness and warmth filled Martin so full that he rose from his chair as if he were floating. This was what he had wanted so much he hadn't dared to hope. He didn't look back. He walked across into the other room . . .

Mrs Collins heard the scream of the ambulance siren as it sped up to the flats on the hill. The still figure lay on the ground where a crowd of neighbours and passers-by had gathered. Everyone could tell there was nothing to be done. Three floors up were too high to fall from and live. What on earth had the boy been doing?

The siren made Mrs Collins remember what she had been trying to think of the other day.

"That happened on Christmas Eve too. Filthy war!" she said aloud.

In her mind's eye she saw the figure of the little red-headed boy again, lying amongst the rubble and twisted girders like a discarded toy. He looked a bit like . . . Same red hair. No one knew him – he hadn't been living there. No one ever knew. Odd, wasn't it?

THE CHIME CHILD

Ian Strachan

yself, I've never believed in ghosts. To me they're as unlikely as snow on Christmas Day – in other words, against all reasonable odds. But what happened to a young friend of mine last year has certainly left me wondering.

Tired of all the commercialisation of Christmas, her father had decided that they should have a totally different kind of celebration and had rented "The Old Parsonage" for them to stay in, buried deep in the Suffolk countryside.

My friend, Christy, due to celebrate her thirteenth birthday that particular Christmas Day, thought it was a boring idea and would much rather have spent time with her friends.

But Dad was adamant, and two nights before Christmas her parents stuffed the car with everything, including Christy's seven-year-old sister Emily, their dog Sam, a Christmas tree and loads of presents.

Of course they should have known better than to set out

when heavy snow began to fall even before they'd left London. But Dad would not turn back. Even when they left the A1 and discovered that strong crosswinds were making it next to impossible to see through the driving snow and huge drifts were piling up, he still refused to give in.

"We're more than halfway there," he pointed out. "It'd be far worse trying to go all the way back."

At last, after a journey that had taken them twice as long as it would have normally, they arrived, exhausted, in a howling blizzard outside a crumbling old pile of a house, already buried up to its window-sills in snow.

"We'll only take essentials for now," Mum shouted as she climbed out into the howling wind, "and unpack the rest in daylight."

Christy rescued Emily, who was almost blown over sideways as the enormous bag she was carrying got caught in the full force of the crosswind.

Dad, using their only torch, found the key according to the instructions, hidden under the doormat in the porch, and unlocked the door.

"For a second," Christy told me later, "when the door was first opened, it smelled as if someone had broken a bad egg into a pair of old trainers. It was as if we'd released something that had been trapped inside."

Mum had dismissed it. "The place probably needs a good airing."

"Then Sam, who's normally a bit of a wimp but doesn't care who he knocks over to be first to get out of bad weather, sat in the drive doing an impersonation of a miserable husky."

The final straw came when Mum tried to put the lights on. The click of the switch echoed round the hall, but nothing happened.

"Maybe it's switched off at the mains, or a fuse has blown," Dad suggested as he went in search of the fuse box. He took the torch with him, leaving the others huddled together, shivering in the pitch-black hall.

Moments later he returned, shaking his head. "Everything's switched on and I've checked all the fuses. The wind must have brought down the power cables. We'll just have to manage without electricity for the time being."

Mum sighed. "That means there's no heat, and unless we can get that old stove going, we can't even boil a kettle for a hot drink."

"I've found some candles," Dad said from the depths of a cupboard he was exploring under the sink.

So that was how they went to bed that first night: carrying candles stuck in saucers up to rooms so cold their breath hung in clouds, and scrambling, half-dressed, into damp beds.

"Well, you got your wish, Dad," Christy muttered to herself through chattering teeth. She lay in bed, watching the distorted shadows the guttering candle projected across her bedroom ceiling. "This really will be a *very* different sort of Christmas!"

*   *   *

Things had improved a little the following morning. The wind had dropped, it had stopped snowing and a watery sun was shining.

Mum had managed to get the Aga going. With the coal shovel Dad had dug a path out to the car, which was buried up to its radiator in snow, and returned with some of their provisions.

By the time Christy wandered into the kitchen, unwashed and frozen to her bones, it was filled with the mouthwatering smell of bacon and fried bread.

Even so, Christy and her mother were determined not to stay, Mum for purely practical reasons. "We've almost used up all their candles and there's only one torch with no spare batteries."

Christy couldn't really put into words what she felt but she was positive she wanted to get as far away from the house as possible. Even if she could have explained her feelings, Dad wouldn't have listened. He was totally carried away with enthusiasm for staying, at all costs.

"Almost all the rooms have got fireplaces," he argued. "I've found a storeroom round the back, full of logs. The place will soon warm up and there's an old paraffin lamp in the sitting room which might give us enough light. After all, this is supposed to be an old-fashioned Christmas. What can be better than sitting round a log fire, singing carols by lamplight?"

"We've got to stay," Emily wailed. "I told Father Christmas I'd be here and he won't find me otherwise."

Christy's scornful reply died on her lips as a huge shadow passed over the window behind them.

"What was that?" she gasped.

They all jumped and Sam barked as somebody banged heavily on the back door.

Dad returned with an absolute mountain of a woman. Her size was further increased by three coats, several scarves, and a big peaked, red balaclava with a shaggy bobble on top. She dumped two bulging carrier bags on the kitchen table, making the cutlery rattle.

"I'm Mrs Pargeter," she announced in a loud voice. "I look after this place. I just popped over to see you'd got here safely and to bring you a few things I thought you might need."

She unloaded six bottles of milk, a dozen eggs and three loaves of bread.

"That's very kind of you," Mum said, "but to be honest we were thinking of going home again."

"You'll not make it!" Mrs Pargeter said bluntly.

"But you got here," Mum pointed out.

"I came over the fields," Mrs Pargeter said, hitching her huge bosom back into place. "Some of the roads are blocked up to the hedge tops and it'll be days before the snowplough comes round here. They never bother with the lanes until they've done all the main roads."

"Looks as if we don't have much choice in the matter," Dad said smugly.

Christy groaned.

"You'll all be a lot safer here than trying to get back," Mrs Pargeter went on. "Mind you, I doubt the electricity'll be back this side of Christmas. There's power cables down all over the place. But you're lucky. That old Aga'll keep in all night."

"If we're going to stay," Mum said doubtfully, "there are quite a few extra things we'll need."

"Get anything you want in the village. Four shops and a Post Office," Mrs Pargeter said proudly.

"But how can we get there?"

"Same way as I got here. Shanks's Pony. Walk across the fields." Mrs Pargeter explained the route. "Follow my footprints to the farm, then look for the church tower and head for that. The village is only a step from there. Well, I'd best be off back."

Mum walked with her to the door. "Will you come again tomorrow?"

Christy thought Mrs Pargeter looked slightly uncomfortable, as if there was something she was trying to avoid saying. "Christmas Eve? No, I'll not set foot in here again till Christmas is over. Mind you, I might see you at the late-night Christmas Eve service. You do go to Church, don't you?"

"Oh, yes!" Mum lied.

"Could be rather nice, that," Dad said thoughtfully, as he watched Mrs Pargeter galumphing across the yard, "a midnight carol service."

*   *   *

Mum's thoughts had already turned to making a shopping list, and half an hour later Christy and her Dad set out, tracking Mrs Pargeter's enormous footsteps across the fields. Although in places they were knee-deep in snow, they passed the Pargeters' farm and easily made it to the church as the clock in the tower struck eleven.

As they passed the graveyard, the rows of snow covered tombstones appeared to Christy like beds in a dormitory, whose occupants had casually thrown back the sheets before climbing out.

The village turned out to be a collection of houses which had sprung up round a T-junction. The shops Mrs Pargeter had mentioned consisted of a small supermarket, a green-grocer, a butcher and an ironmonger's. With the roads deep in snow no traffic moved and the village was eerily silent. What cars there were stood parked by the kerb like rows of white blancmanges.

Most of the pavements had been cleared, though one or two late risers were still shovelling away. None bothered to stop as Christy and her Dad walked by, but Christy had an uneasy feeling, a prickle in the back of her neck, that the villagers turned to stare after them the moment they'd passed.

Dad tore a piece off the shopping list and handed it, together with some money, to Christy. "I'll do the super-market if you do the ironmonger's."

The paint on the ironmonger's window was dark green, cracked and peeling, though the display was stuffed with everything from shiny modern garden implements to paraffin heaters.

A bell jangled above her head as Christy opened the door. Inside the dark shop she breathed a heady mixture of paraffin, polish and garden fertiliser.

"Morning!" said a tiny, bird-like man in a reedy voice. He had dark beady eyes and sat perched behind the counter on a low set of folding steps. "You'll be staying at the Old Parsonage."

Christy, who had lived all her life in London where next-door neighbours can remain strangers, was surprised at being so easily identified. "Yes."

"Plenty of people stay there in the summer, but I reckon you'll be the first ever to stay over Christmas."

Christy wasn't certain what to make of that news. "Oh."

"Just that most people prefer to keep away from there during Christmas."

"Mrs Pargeter said something like that."

The man leant over the counter confidentially and whispered, as if he was afraid the packets of soap-powder might overhear, "Did she tell you why?" Christy shook her head. "'Tis only a story. I don't reckon there's any truth in it, but they do say that just before Christmas, hundreds of years ago, a little girl was walled up somewhere in that house by her wicked uncle and left to die a slow, terrible death."

Christy felt a shiver run down her spine. "Ugh! How horrible."

The man looked even more birdlike as he cocked his head

on one side and peered up at her with narrowed eyes. "I suppose you haven't heard anything unusual up there? Noises, or anything?"

"You don't mean there's a ghost?"

"I don't suppose you believe in ghosts?"

"No, of course not," Christy said firmly. A thought struck her. "Anyway, the Old Parsonage isn't hundreds of years old."

"Ah, no," the man agreed. "After the child died the house fell down. The Church built the Parsonage on to the only bit left standing. Mrs Pargeter tells me it's easy to see which is which. The back is much older than the front. But," he said, changing the subject abruptly, "I can't spend all morning gossiping. What do you want?"

Christy, who had long since forgotten her original errand, fumbled in her pocket for the list. But while she asked for candles, firelighters and batteries, her mind was really on the poor girl and the gruesome end she'd suffered!

"Is that everything?" the man asked, starting to tot up the cost on the back of an envelope.

"Oh, one more thing – birthday cake candles. Mum forgot to bring any."

"Christmas cake you mean, don't you?" the man corrected her, reaching for a small packet of pink candles.

"Well, both really. Christmas Day's my birthday, just."

The man looked sharply at her. "What do you mean 'just'?"

"Mum always says she thought I was going to happen on

193

Christmas Eve, but in the end I was born on the last stroke of
midnight. So I came on Christmas Day. Which is why they
called me Christy."

"The last stroke of midnight," the man said thoughtfully.
"Then you're very special aren't you?"

"Special?"

"You're what's known round here as a Chime Child."

"What's a Chime Child?"

"It's said, anyone born while the clock is chiming the magi-
cal hours of three, six, nine or twelve has special powers."

Christy couldn't resist asking, "Like what?"

"They do say they have power over animals."

Christy laughed. "I can't even persuade our dog not to
sleep on my bed."

The shopkeeper sighed. "I see you don't believe in our
funny little ways. But there are things you should know, for
your own safety."

"Such as?"

"All Chime Children are supposed to be gifted with a
knowledge of herbs and herbal healing and be protected from
ill-wishing, but those born at midnight are also said to be able
to see ghosts and talk to them."

Christy felt her throat dry up. "You mean, if there was a
ghost in the Old Parsonage *I* would be the one most likely to
see it?"

"But you said you don't believe in ghosts, so that's hardly
likely to be a problem, is it? That'll be eight pounds ninety-
five."

Outside, blinking in the sunlight, the conversation she'd had with the shopkeeper seemed unreal to Christy. Only the purchases in the carrier bag convinced her that it had ever really happened.

Dad didn't help, coming up behind her. "You look as if you'd seen a ghost," he said.

She jumped and smiled weakly. "Something like that. Have we got everything? I'd like to go back."

"The only thing I haven't got is mistletoe."

The woman in the greengrocer's shook her head. "Bless you, I'm afraid we never stock mistletoe. Nobody in the village buys it. The stuff grows wild on the old apple and ash trees round here, so they can get it for nothing. You're staying in the Old Parsonage, aren't you?"

Christy smiled. Everyone seemed to know who they were.

"I'd have thought you'd have known all about the mistletoe then," she added, looking straight at Christy. "Well," she went on, "you passed some on the way here. It grows all over that big old oak tree, the one just off the path between the Parsonage and the Pargeters' farm. You could cut some on the way back."

It was only when they were back in the kitchen, unloading the shopping, and Mum asked, "And where's the mistletoe?" that they realised they'd forgotten to look out for the tree and had returned without any.

One reason it was forgotten was that, all the way back,

Christy had been wondering whether to tell her father any of the strange things the ironmonger had said.

The trouble was, out there in the fresh air, walking through the crisp snow, it all sounded so stupid. Who could possibly believe all that nonsense about the ghost of a long-dead child? And as for there being anything special about a Chime Child . . .!

Even so, Christy took the first opportunity she got to explore the whole house properly. In daylight and with fires lit in all the downstairs rooms, the house was not only a good deal warmer, but it looked and felt more cheerful too. That impression was helped by the Christmas decorations Emily and Mum had put up. They'd also dressed the tree, which stood in a bay window of the sitting room.

She found it was quite easy to tell which was the old part of the house. On the landing an arch led off to the bathroom and the polished floorboards suddenly dipped where the two parts did not quite make a perfect join.

In a corridor in the same part of the house downstairs Christy found that the old stone of the wall had been left exposed. The plaster ended on either side in two huge, upright, blackened beams. A gilt-framed oil painting of some rather damp-looking sheep on a bleak hillside hung crookedly in the centre of the wall and beneath it was a large oak chest.

Though the stones were of irregular sizes, their ends were so smooth they almost looked as if they'd been polished, and they all keyed neatly together.

Neatly, except for the centre.

From above the picture, a narrow crack ran right down the middle of the wall, finally disappearing behind the chest.

"Oh, that picture!" Mum said crossly, as she came past and adjusted the frame. "I've put that right twenty times this morning and every time I come back it's crooked again!"

Christy got her father to look at the wall. "Part of it's wet," she said, showing him her hand, still damp from where she'd touched the stone.

Dad shrugged. "Condensation, I expect. You get it in old houses, especially when they heat up after being left empty."

On an impulse, Christy licked her fingers. "This tastes salty, like tears. Almost as if the wall is crying."

Dad smiled. "More likely to be salts leaching out of the old stones."

Christy wasn't convinced. "What do you think's on the other side of this wall?"

"The storeroom where I got the logs for the Aga."

Christy heaved a quiet sigh of relief. At least there could be no walled-in skeleton crouched in a secret recess.

However, next time she passed the wall the picture of the sheep was crooked again. Worse still, she was convinced that the crack running through the stones had widened.

"I'm positive," she said, taking her father to examine it.

"And I'm sure you're wrong," he said, "but there's only

one way to prove it." He produced a roll of sellotape which he'd been using while wrapping presents. "We'll stick a length of this across the crack, high up where it's dry. Then if anything moves, the tape will break."

The family went to bed early that night. They had discovered there was a limit to what they could do sitting round a single oil lamp. Besides, when the temperature outside dropped below freezing again the log fire didn't feel nearly as warm to people used to central heating.

In spite of a hot-water bottle, by the time Christy had thrown off her clothes, jumped into bed and blown out her candle, she was frozen and missed the comforting, furry body of Sam stretched out beside her. They had managed to tempt him as far as the kitchen, where he'd spent the day curled up beside the Aga, but he wouldn't go any further. Christy had tried to encourage him to go up with her, but he'd crouched down, growling, his hackles raised, when they reached the stone wall.

"Sam! Don't be silly," she had said, grabbing his collar and trying to tug him along. But he braced himself so firmly that she'd given up and let him back into the kitchen, where he bolted under the huge scrub-topped table.

Eventually Christy drifted off into an uneasy sleep, only to be woken by the sound of Sam howling.

As nobody else seemed to have heard him she lit her candle. The cold bit into her the moment her feet were out of bed and she threw on a thick sweater as well as her anorak. Slowly, in case the draught should blow out the candle's fluttering flame, she crept down the twisting staircase.

As she opened the kitchen door Sam's head poked out from under the table. He whimpered a greeting, his tail thumping against the tiled floor, but refused to come towards her. When she tried to get closer he backed away and began scratching furiously at the back door.

Christy, feeling sorry for him, unlocked the door. It was barely open when Sam forced his way through and disappeared into the darkness.

She heated some milk, expecting to share it with Sam when he returned, but he didn't. She waited. Twice she opened the door and called, but there was no sign of him. As she locked up, noticing that it was snowing heavily again, she hoped he'd found shelter in one of the outbuildings.

It was as she was passing the stone wall on her way back to bed that she heard the child sobbing. At first she thought it must be Emily, but her sister was upstairs and this sounded much closer.

"Who's there?" she asked quietly, holding the candle aloft with a shaking hand.

Silence.

Wondering if she'd imagined it, Christy took another step towards the stairs but the sobbing began again.

"Who *is* that?" There was a short pause, but still no reply and then the sobbing resumed, this time accompanied by faint moans.

Now she knew where it came from. It was as if somebody was crouched down on the floor behind the oak chest at the base of the stone wall.

"Why are you doing this to me?" Christy asked desperately. She stood waiting, by now shivering with cold and fear, but nothing else happened.

But as she held the candle closer to the wall, she saw the sellotape Dad had stuck across the crack had been ripped apart and the fracture was much wider.

Although no more sounds disturbed that night, Christy spent it sitting on her bed with the candle lit, huddled in blankets and hugging her pillow. Not until daylight seeped through the chinks in the heavy velvet curtains did she allow herself to drift off into an uneasy sleep.

The first footfall on the landing woke Christy and she found her father going downstairs.

"Did you hear anything in the night?" she demanded.

Dad looked puzzled. "No, why?"

Broad daylight made Christy begin to feel foolish. She shrugged. "I had to get up to Sam. He was howling his head off. He insisted on being let out."

"Silly old thing. Did he come back?"

Christy shook her head.

"I shouldn't worry – he'll have found himself a cosy nook somewhere. Animals often behave oddly in strange places. He'll soon get used to it."

"And then I . . ." Christy was about to tell him about the sobbing, but changed her mind, " . . .I noticed the sellotape you put over the crack had broken."

"Really?" Dad, pleased that his idea had worked, went to examine it. "So it has."

"The crack's much wider now."

Hearing the concern in Christy's voice, he slid an arm round her shoulder. "There's nothing to worry about. These old places aren't built on very firm foundations – there's always a certain amount of settlement. Maybe the cold weather's brought it on. But it's stood up for about a hundred years, so I'm sure it won't fall down this week. Come on, it's freezing out here! Let's go in the kitchen and get a good hot drink."

The rest of the family's thoughts were on their final preparations for Christmas. Emily was positively bursting now that, at long last, Christmas Eve had arrived.

During the morning, Dad asked Christy to bring in some logs. She was about to load a basket in the stone storeroom at the back of the house, when she realised that it seemed much shallower than the bathroom above.

Dropping the basket, she ran into the house.

"What's up?" Dad asked as she hared through the kitchen. "Where are the logs?"

"Back in a minute!" she called over her shoulder.

Once in the bathroom she paced it out. Three strides in either direction.

She ran past her bewildered father, back to the storeroom.

Though the logs made it impossible to pace out properly, the storeroom was obviously as wide as the bathroom but definitely much shallower – a difference of a metre and a half. Easily enough room for a body.

Unnerved by her discovery, she took the logs back and dropped them beside the Aga. "Dad, I've just done some measuring and the bathroom above is much bigger than the storeroom – about a metre and a half."

Dad continued peeling potatoes. "That's not surprising. It isn't easy to build a stone wall and they don't keep in much heat, so they're often very thick."

Christy subsided.

"What's so important about that anyway?"

She shook her head. "Nothing. It doesn't matter." Yet another fascinating theory had been dismissed.

That afternoon, as the storm outside grew more fierce, Christy went up to her bedroom to finish some last-minute present-wrapping. There, glancing along a shelf of dusty old books, she noticed an old local guide book, discoloured by damp and age. Leafing through the pages she found:

Old Parsonage:
The present Victorian building was erected on the site of a much older stone structure which may have dated back to the 13th century.

The superstitious insist the Old Parsonage has a ghost.

Thirteen-year-old Rachel Soame, whose parents were

killed in a coaching accident, came to live in the original house during the Civil War. It belonged to Rachel's Uncle, Ezra Be-Thankful Dexter, a Puritan like most people in the area. Ezra Dexter had strong political ambitions and, to further these, he wanted to get his hands on Rachel's inheritance.

Rachel had, unfortunately, fallen deeply in love with a Catholic boy, Benedict Salinger, something which, if it became known, would seriously damage her uncle's plans. He forbade Rachel to see Benedict, but she persisted.

Shortly before Christmas in the year 1643, Rachel disappeared and rumour got about that Ezra had walled up his poor niece somewhere in the house and left her to die.

However, Ezra's ambitions were frustrated when he could not find the Will he had forced the girl to write in his favour. He mounted a desperate search for the document, which only ended after he had torn down all but a small part of the house – the part, they say, where Rachel's remains lay.

Ezra Be-Thankful Dexter, who many believed became possessed by the Devil, ended his days "still consumed with wickedness and a burning lust for money and power" in an asylum for the insane.

For years, until the present building was erected, the house lay ruined. It is called the Old Parsonage *because the new incumbent lived there only briefly, finding it "disquieting", and yet another parsonage was built, more convenient to the village.*

As Christy put the book aside with a shudder, a clatter of hail on the window made her look up, and as she did so the force of the wind blew the window open.

Christy was aware of a violent rush of air entering the room. The blast was far stronger than the wind itself. Nor was it fresh air. It carried a foul stench which reminded her of the night they'd arrived when the front door was first unlocked, but far worse. With difficulty she shut the window and raced downstairs.

Dad met her in the corridor. "I thought that smell would bring you out of your hiding place," he said.

"You noticed it too?" At last, she thought, somebody else was sharing one of the sensations she'd been suffering alone.

"I think baking bread gives off the most wonderful smell in the world," Dad smiled.

"Baking bread?"

"Surely you can smell it?"

Christy sniffed. Above the horrible odour that still lingered in her nostrils, she could detect the first whiff of the aroma her father was savouring. "Yes, I can," she said, turning back to the stairs.

"It'll be out of the oven in a moment. Aren't you staying for some?"

"In a moment," she murmured.

As she went back to her room, Christy wondered if she was simply making something out of nothing, or if she was going mad. The crumbling wall, Sam's fear of the house, that hideous smell – why was she experiencing all these things, while the rest of the family carried on as usual, unaware of anything strange?

"Because I'm a Chime Child!" she said sarcastically to herself. "What a load of rubbish!"

But was it? Hadn't the ironmonger told her that a Chime Child was supposed to be aware of things other people were not?

By evening, when they set out for the carol service, the worst of the storm had passed. Most of the village seemed to be there, including the ironmonger, the greengrocer and Mrs Pargeter.

The church was beautifully decorated and for the first time since they'd arrived in the village Christy felt comfortable. She enjoyed the service, especially singing the familiar carols and hearing the clock above them strike midnight.

Afterwards Christy's mum and dad smiled and nodded at the villagers who were standing, chatting, around the main door. They had moved on down the path with Emily when Mrs Pargeter touched Christy's hand.

"I just wanted to say, we're all very glad you've come."

Assuming she was referring to the family, Christy smiled. "Thank you. We enjoyed the service very much."

"Oh, no. I meant that you'd come to the Old Parsonage for Christmas. *You* particularly."

Something about the way she stressed the word brought

back all Christy's uncertainty, but she managed to say, politely, "I'm sure we'll all enjoy it."

A cloud passed briefly over Mrs Pargeter's broad features. "I hope you do," she said earnestly and then hurriedly left Christy to rejoin her husband.

Christy ran down the path to catch up with the others, who had already gone through the lychgate. As she pulled back the catch on the gate she noticed a figure lurking in the shadow of the arch. She drew back, but his voice was comforting. "Don't be afraid, I'm only here to offer help."

"Who are you?"

"One of an Ancient Order of Druids." A shaft of moonlight briefly pierced the scudding clouds and revealed a tall figure, dressed in long flowing robes with a hood which hid his face. He stretched out a hand towards her. When he opened it Christy jumped, for a knife lay in his palm. The Druid said quietly, "Take it."

Cautiously she obeyed. About fifteen centimetres long, both its blade and the ornately carved handle, which were made of the same yellow metal, appeared to glow. "Is it gold?" Christy asked.

The cowled head nodded. "Remember, to retain the power, cut only with this."

Staring at the knife in her hand, Christy demanded, "Cut what? What power? What are you talking about?"

But when she looked up the figure had disappeared.

"Come on, Christy – we're all waiting!" her father called from the field path.

She hurriedly thrust the knife into her anorak pocket and ran to catch up.

"Happy birthday, darling!" Mum said, giving her a big hug which Dad and Emily joined in.

Christy smiled. "It never feels like my birthday until I've been to sleep."

Back at the house, Mum made them all hot drinks, but Emily was too excited to touch hers. Instead she danced round the kitchen, bubbling over at the prospect of hanging up her stocking and opening her presents. Eventually Mum gave in and let her open one before going to bed.

Emily ripped open the parcel and waved a cuddly penguin in the air. "Look what I've got!" she shouted, and then immediately asked if she could open another one.

"No," said Dad, scooping her up in his arms and leading the way upstairs.

As they passed the stone wall, Christy could have sworn she heard a trickle of mortar running down the back, as if one of the huge stones had shifted.

A deep, slow rumble followed by a loud crash woke Christy. The noise had come from the corridor below. Lighting her candle, she quickly dressed in sweater and jeans and made her way down.

Dust hung thickly in the corridor. Through it she saw that the stone wall had collapsed completely, burying the oak chest.

Christy peered over the rubble into the darkness beyond. She saw a small empty room – no skeleton, just a bare, dusty stone floor.

As she stood staring she became aware of a force drawing her towards the sitting room. The pull was too strong to resist and she gave in to it, walking as if in a trance.

She opened the door. There, crouched on the hearth and shivering beside the dying embers, was a girl of Christy's age. She wore a plain white nightdress and her arms and legs were painfully thin. Her crow-black hair emphasised the deathly whiteness of her skin.

There was no doubt in Christy's mind that this was poor, wretched Rachel Soame.

Two things surprised Christy. The first was how solid Rachel seemed; the second was that Rachel appeared to be more afraid than she was, though not of Christy.

"Christy! I thought you were never coming. I've waited so long for your help," said the girl.

"I came when you cried the other night. Why didn't you answer?"

"That was too soon."

"What can *I* do?"

"You have been sent to use your special powers against the spirit of my uncle Ezra."

Christy shook her head, baffled. "I don't understand. If you're both . . ." she was about to say "dead" but changed her mind, "If you're both ghosts, how can you harm each other any more?"

"Because he is filled with the Devil's power. For centuries he has tried to drag me down with him into never-ending torment. Only when he is finally despatched can I be truly free of this place and join my beloved Benedict in everlasting happiness."

Christy felt helpless. "But I won't know what to do."

"You *will* know when the time comes, and that will be soon."

"How do you know?"

"I died at four o'clock in the morning of the fifteenth of December," Rachel said in a matter-of-fact way.

"Then you're safe!" Christy cried. "It's Christmas Day, the twenty-fifth of December. So your anniversary's passed."

Rachel slowly shook her head. "No, you forget. Some hundred years after my death the calendar was changed and the fifteenth became Christmas Day. Uncle Ezra holds to the old calendar. Year after year he seeks me out at the exact time of my death. Each year I evade him but this year, knowing of your presence, I have risked coming out to confront him. If I am not to be destroyed, you must equip yourself. Your spiritual power is in no doubt, but there is something else you need – mistletoe. Since the dawn of time it has had mystical powers of protection against evil."

"But there's none in the house!" Christy exclaimed in panic. She glanced at her watch. Half past three.

"Go swiftly!" Rachel urged. "Collect a branch and bring it back to the house. Go now – there's not a second to lose!"

"I'm not sure I'll be able to find the tree in all the snow."

"Be led by your heart," Rachel said earnestly, "but above all be swift."

Christy raced out to the kitchen, pulled on boots and her anorak, grabbed her father's torch and drew back the bolts.

Sam barked but did not show himself as she ran across the slippery stones of the yard, heading for the path towards the farm.

Although it wasn't snowing, the fierce, icy wind was whipping up the powdery snow in blinding clouds, which covered her tracks immediately and created more and deeper drifts.

The weakening beam of the torch failed to penetrate the murk. Christy only had the slightest idea which direction she should take and stumbled several times as she struggled through the snow.

The woman in the greengrocer's had mentioned a big oak tree off the path between the Pargeters' farm and the Old Parsonage. But how was she to find it? The snow had smothered the entire landscape until one thing looked much like another. Rachel's advice, "Be led by your heart", was all very well, but time was running out and all Christy could feel in her heart was fear.

Cold, damp and frightened, she staggered on until she made out the shape of the Pargeters' farm. "Oh, no!" she cried angrily. "That means I've gone too far!"

She turned back, searching more carefully but found nothing tall enough to be a tree. Her leg suddenly sank deep into a drift. Beneath the snow her foot caught a stone, slipped off and pitched her forward to land with a stunning thump on something very solid.

She must have been briefly unconscious because the next thing she remembered was coming round, as if from a deep sleep. The curious part was that she felt no inclination to get up.

The cruel wind began to cover Christy's body with a light covering of snow and she started to merge into the land-scape . . .

The church clock rescued her. Just as she was floating off into a comforting sleep, Christy faintly heard the three-quarter hour striking. She realised with a start there were only fifteen minutes left before Ezra would attack Rachel.

Grabbing the torch, she struggled to her feet. Feverishly brushing off the life-threatening snow, she noticed something clinging to the cuff of her anorak. It looked like a tiny pearl, then she realised, "It's a mistletoe berry!"

The solid object on which she had struck her head must have been the trunk of the old oak tree, brought down by a combination of tremendous winds and the enormous weight of wet snow clinging to its branches.

Christy dropped to her knees and began frantically digging with her bare hands, deep into the bank of snow. Her fingers ached but she knew she must not stop.

Slowly, dark, gnarled branches emerged. "But where's

211

the mistletoe?" she wailed. "Maybe this isn't even the right tree."

At long last she came across a single, pale green, oval leaf. Further digging revealed a branch of mistletoe, still entwined round the oak, sucking the last drops of sap from the host tree's dying branches.

Christy grabbed the smooth-skinned, golden-green branch and tried to pull it free. But the limb was very pliable and no matter how far she bent it, or how hard she tugged, it refused to break. The Druid's words came back to her. "To retain the power, cut only with this."

Christy felt in her pocket, frightened she might have dropped the knife as she stumbled through the snow.

Her hand grasped its carved hilt and by the dying light of the torch, she put the golden blade to the branch. The knife cut through the wood as if it were an oar parting water. For a few moments, as the final strand of bark split and it separated from the oak, the mistletoe gave off a golden glow – a glow which seemed to come right from the core of the wood.

The search for the mistletoe had been bad enough, but the return journey proved even worse. The torch battery soon gave out and Christy trudged on blindly, fearing she might be walking in circles, until suddenly, above the roar of the wind, she heard a familiar sound. From her left came the distinctive sound of Sam's howling.

Using Sam as a homing beacon, Christy took off as fast as she could and discovered to her surprise that in her moment of deepest despair she had been only metres away from the Old Parsonage.

Sam stopped the moment Christy set foot in the yard but, although she made much of him for rescuing her, he refused to go nearer the house but slunk away to hide in one of the outbuildings.

The house stood dark and totally silent. Christy hastily lit a hurricane lamp and checked her watch. Gone four. Perhaps she was already too late? Cautiously she made her way towards the sitting room.

Without warning Christy suddenly felt herself hurled backwards against the wall as some strong, invisible force swept by her, accompanied again by the hideous, rank odour.

She ran into the sitting-room. Rachel lay motionless on the hearthrug in front of the almost dead fire, half-hidden by the settee. Her face was pale and drawn, her lips blue with cold. Her eyelids fluttered weakly at Christy's approach and her lips parted. "I thought you were never coming. Uncle Ezra is near," she murmured. "I can feel his presence drawing away my strength."

"What do I do with the mistletoe now that I've got it?" Christy asked.

"First, cut a sprig for me to hold. If all else fails that will be my final hope."

Christy did as she was told and Rachel clutched it in both hands on her chest. "Use the golden knife to put a sharp point on the end of the main branch. You must drive it into his heart."

Christy's hand shook with fear at the thought while she pared off the bark. She had just finished when she heard the wordless roar of a man's voice. Though it seemed to come from outside, it was so loud it enveloped the house.

An ominous rumble of thunder shook the walls and the smell of fetid decay grew stronger as a gaseous, luminous green light filtered into the room.

Ezra Be-Thankful Dexter stood, framed by the open door, every bit as substantial as Rachel. He was a short, fat man dressed in faded black. His hair, cut in the Parliamentarian style, hung in grey rats' tails about his podgy face, from which his two piercing green eyes looked out.

"Rachel!" he shouted. "Your time has come. This year I *will* take you back with me!"

Christy was quivering, but she managed to say, haltingly, "No, you won't."

Ezra swung round on her. "Who are you, boy?"

"I'm a girl, and my name is Christy."

"What kind of girl, to shamelessly expose herself in men's clothes?" He dismissed her with a curt wave of his arm. "Whoever you be, these things don't concern you. I warn you, leave my affairs alone." He took a step towards Rachel. "Come, child. You can deny me no longer."

"Don't touch her," Christy said quietly.

Ezra slowly turned, eyes blazing, his face twisted with rage. "I've warned you once, now hold your peace!"

"Haven't you already harmed Rachel enough? Leave her alone."

214

"If you will not heed me, I must needs teach you a lesson."

The hand he extended towards Christy looked deformed until she realised he was holding his fingers in a curious formation. The middle finger was folded under both the thumb and little finger, leaving the other two pointing directly at her head. "Feel this!" he shouted.

With a sharp crackle, a bolt of blue-green light burst from his finger-ends. Christy felt something like a hammer-blow hit her as she crashed backwards into the furniture.

Badly dazed, she tried to shake her head but found she couldn't. Worse, she could see that the branch of mistletoe she'd been holding behind her had dropped on the floor and been kicked under the settee.

Helpless, she watched while the evil old man waddled towards Rachel. She tried to call out, but her tongue seemed to have grown too large for her mouth and she could only manage a burble of sound that sent a dribble of spittle trickling down her chin. She tried to wipe it away but all the power had ebbed from her muscles.

Ezra read the panic in her eyes and gave a grim smile, but his expression changed when he bent over Rachel and saw the mistletoe she was clutching. He turned back on Christy. "Is this your doing?"

Christy tried to nod but her head fell forwards on her chest and it took an enormous effort of will for her to lift it again.

"You meddle with things you cannot begin to understand," he warned her. "Powers from the Old Days, of mystic superstition that were best forgotten."

As his hand brushed against the mistletoe he leapt back, clutching himself as if scalded.

Taking the long brass poker from the hearth, Ezra tried dislodge the mistletoe from Rachel's weakening grasp, but the poker glowed white-hot and he dropped it onto the fireplace with a howl of anguish.

"It seems," Ezra said with a snarl, as he shuffled across to Christy, "that what you have done, you must now undo."

He thrust his face close to hers and Christy smelt the foul breath which oozed from between his broken, yellowing teeth.

The numbness which had soaked through her limbs prevented her from escaping yet, to her own surprise, she found she had regained the power of speech. "Keep away from me," she said defiantly.

"Stop telling me what to do!" he commanded. "You have no authority, but you *will* be useful to me."

His eyes seemed to bore deep inside Christy and she became aware that the use was slowly returning to her muscles, although her veins seemed to be filled with ice.

"Come with me," he said, dragging her towards Rachel.

He did not have to pull hard. Though the paralysis had gone her legs and arms remained weaker than a rag doll's. Besides, he had a hypnotic power which compelled her to obey.

He ordered Christy to kneel beside Rachel. "Take off that vile thing!"

Against her will, Christy was about to remove the sprig of mistletoe when, out of the corner of her eye, she saw the sharpened end of the branch from which it had been cut, poking out from beneath the settee.

Unaware of her thoughts, Ezra roared, "Do it, girl!"

Christy remained frozen. She could feel a tremendous battle raging between her own will and his. Even as her hand reached out for the branch, something unseen prevented her from touching it.

She tried again. This time, with an enormous effort, she forced her hand through the invisible wall. She grasped the branch and felt warmth flowing back into her body. With one swift movement she pulled the branch from its hiding place and sprang up, brandishing it.

"Don't think to threaten me," Ezra warned, but his face paled and his hands trembled.

He rushed at her and without thinking, Christy hit him with the only thing available – the mistletoe.

The result was astounding. The branch caught him where his arm joined the shoulder. As it struck there was a vivid, golden flash, a rank smell of flesh burning and Christy watched in horror as Ezra's hand and arm sizzled and withered in its sleeve.

He leapt back with an agonised scream and then, with his remaining hand, attempted to aim another bolt of green lightning at her.

She ducked behind her only shield, the mistletoe. Though the branch rattled in her hand beneath the impact, the lightning was deflected, as if by a mirror, into a far corner of the room.

Realising the power she held, Christy began to pursue him, making certain that she kept the branch between them, lunging at him with the vicious point.

He fended her off by hurling vases, paperweights and framed photographs, but Christy began to sense victory.

They circled the room, knocking over the Christmas tree and scattering presents, until she had him cornered beside the fireplace. There was only a stride between them and she was about to drive the stake into his body when he snatched up a little stool. Lifting it high above his head, he brought it crashing down on Christy.

She staggered back, sprawling on the floor close to Rachel. As she fell, she knocked over the hurricane lamp and the spilt paraffin burst into flames. Too late, she realised that she had again lost the mistletoe.

Ezra sprang stiffly over the branch to prevent her retrieving it. "Aha! I have you!" he snarled. "Now we'll play this game my way. Get that filthy stuff away from Rachel!"

The flames dancing round her, Christy grabbed the sprig from Rachel's hands. As she did, she remembered the golden knife, and while she hurled the mistletoe at Ezra, she snatched it from her pocket.

The mistletoe caught him full in the face, leaving a livid imprint on his skin. He cried out in agony, staggered forward clutching his injured face, tripped over the rumpled edge of the burning hearth-rug and fell.

As he toppled towards her Christy screamed in terror.

She tried to roll out of the way, but as he landed he was impaled on the golden knife.

She struggled to be free of him and scrambled to her feet. As she watched, transfixed, the body of Ezra Be-Thankful Dexter crumbled away into powder, caught alight and burned with an intense heat until there was nothing left. Nothing but the knife, twisted by the heat and bearing an ugly, green stain on the blade, like verdigris.

Christy was busy beating out the dying flames on the rug with her anorak when Rachel stood up. The despatching of her uncle seemed to have had an immediate effect. Colour was already flooding back into her cheeks. "Thank you," she said.

"What happens now?" Christy asked.

"Only this," Rachel said softly. She took from the pocket of her nightdress a crumpled paper with the single faded word "Will" on it. Rachel dropped the paper onto the fire and watched the charred remains disappear up the chimney.

Then Christy realised the girl was slowly fading away.

Mentally and physically exhausted, Christy collapsed into an armchair and fell into the deepest sleep she had experienced since arriving at the Old Parsonage.

She woke to find her mother bending over her. "Happy birthday again, Christy!" she said. "Thank you for getting up early to bring in some mistletoe, but you really shouldn't have left it lying on the floor."

Bewildered, Christy glanced round the room. There was no sign of the fight, let alone a fire. Broken ornaments and disturbed furniture were all safely back in their original positions and the presents were stacked neatly beneath the tree.

She raced out into the corridor. The stone wall had also been restored without even a hairline crack. The picture hung straight on its hook and there wasn't so much as a scratch on the highly polished surface of the oak chest.

Why? What had happened? Had *anything* happened or had it all been some hideous nightmare brought on by everything she had heard and read about the Old Parsonage?

But then she remembered the mistletoe – that was real enough – and the knife? Slowly Christy unlocked her clenched fingers and raised her right hand. There it lay in her palm gleaming dully, twisted as if by intense heat, its blade disfigured by an ugly green stain.

She stood for a moment longer, gazing at the knife, then she smiled, put it in her pocket, and turned back to join her family in the joy of Christmas and the beginning of a new year in her life.

So now you may understand my uncertainties about the existence of ghosts, especially as, while I've been telling this extraordinary tale the hideously disfigured knife lies before me, but perhaps my doubts are only prompted by the owls hooting close to the house, the desolate barking of the foxes in the wood and the grandfather clock which is chiming Midnight.

CRESPIAN AND CLAIRAN

Joan Aiken

ou ask why I prefer to run a school for drop-outs – for delinquents? Well, I will tell you. Put another log on the fire. My story goes back a long way.

When I was a child (said the headmaster, gazing at the leaping flames) Christmas was the time of year that I hated most. Its arrival always put me in a black mood. And, from that kind of black mood, danger can build up.

My parents, you see, were elderly: he in his fifties, she in her forties when *I* was born – a most unexpected and, I fear, most unwelcome addition to the family. My elder brother was long since off in the world, farming in Canada. My father, a successful writer of scientific textbooks, could live as and where he chose, and what he had chosen, for the past ten years, was to spend a month or so each Christmas in the South of France with my mother. And to take a small

221

tiresome child with them formed no part of this programme. My presence would have ruined their agreeable holiday; in fact it was not to be thought of.

From age four, accordingly – or it may even have been from age three, I was so young that I am not certain to a year when the arrangement first began – I was despatched every Christmas to the north country, to Marwick, to stay with my Aunt Nesta and Uncle Simon and my cousin Becky. Oh, how bitterly I resented this! And as soon as I began going to school I resented it even more. Other children began looking forward to Christmas at home for weeks and months in advance. They had all kinds of joyful family rituals and long-standing practices remembered from year to year, for which they planned and schemed and saved their pocket-money: the flowers for Mother, mincepies and dancing at midnight on Christmas Eve, the conspiratorial filling and hanging-up of stockings, mixing of cakes and puddings, fetching the tree home, singing carols round the piano, decorating the house.

"We always make holly-chains from baskets and baskets of holly leaves threaded on to string," said one girl in my class. "It takes days to make the long ones and oh! how they prick your fingers. It's agony, but they look superb and rich when they are hung up, like tapestries."

"We always take the dog to the beach on Christmas morning for a two-hour walk. Always. Sometimes the sand is frozen, the wind's bitter cold, and it's wonderful to think of the turkey back at home in the oven, getting browner and browner."

"My sisters and I always act a play on Christmas night," said another boy. "It's in verse and it takes weeks to write, and my aunts and uncles and grandparents come to watch; it's a bit silly but I think they'd miss it if we didn't do it. . . ."

Needless to say, nothing of this kind took place in *my* home. The festive season, to my parents, was merely a time to ignore as far as possible, to get through as quietly and inconspicuously as possible. I suppose, even in their villa on the Riviera, it must have been difficult not to be aware of lights, decorations, and seasonal gaieties going on outside, but these need be no concern of theirs; they had their own circle and managed very well in their own matter-of-fact way.

And I, meanwhile, was up at Marwick with my uncle and aunt, my cousin Becky a year older than me, and, presently, her two baby brothers.

Marwick is a bleak, bleak place. On the east coast, it is one of those grey, grim towns that seem to cling to the ground, bracing themselves against the fierce wind that comes scouring in from Siberia. My Uncle Simon's house, a big ugly one, stood on a hillside at the edge of the town. From the top of its high garden wall (necessary to keep the cabbages from blowing out of the ground) you could see Marwick castle, a crumbling ruin, built long ago for defence against marauding Vikings, and the North Sea, a leaden ruled line across the horizon.

All the trees leaned over sideways, as if they wanted to grab hold of the ground; my Aunt Nesta protected her favourite garden plants with glass cloches, and these were continually being blown over and smashed in ferocious gales, so that the garden was a minefield of broken glass where my smaller cousins were never permitted to stray unescorted.

Another hazard was the pond, said to be twenty feet deep. My uncle, manager of a steel foundry in the neighbouring town of Forreskirk, told us that the pond had been used for iron-work in the middle ages. He was fond of history, and used to tell Becky stories about Danes and Norsemen when he took us for walks. I think the pond was one of the reasons why he had bought Kelso House, which was otherwise inconvenient, rambling, much too big, and frightfully cold. The wind whistled through its large, ill-fitting windows and along its uncarpeted corridors.

Becky was delicate. This was one of the many reasons why I disliked her. A pale girl with transparent white skin and guileless grey eyes, she was subject to asthma and bronchial troubles. Her hair, very fair, hung in two plaits like a Viking girl's. Whenever we went outside she had to wrap up with extreme care, putting on layers and layers of wool and covering her neck and ears with hoods and scarves and mufflers. I found this prissy and cissy and thought it was all affectation and probably not needed at all.

I'm afraid it can't be denied that I was a very unpleasant boy: self-centred, intolerant, narrow, almost completely unaware of other people's rights or needs or interests. I was also a thief, as you will presently see. That gives me an insight now . . . I had never been treated with generosity at home, and I saw no occasion to be generous to others.

What other reasons had I for disliking Becky?

Pathetically, *she* was very fond of *me*. This, I suppose, was because she was rather lonely. Often, she would not be considered well enough to go to school and so must stay at home, reading all the books in the house – of which there were hundreds. My Aunt Nesta was a great reader, and was prepared, if ever she had time, to read aloud to us. But she was very busy most of the day, looking after the awkward, badly-equipped house and the two younger boys, who were much too small to be any use in Becky's and my games.

"Oh John, I wish you could stay here all the time," Becky used to say sadly, when my time to leave was approaching and I, for my part, was counting the days, the hours, the minutes. "We have so much more fun when you are here." Poor Becky. Little did she realise how tedious and irritating I often found her.

She was always inventing new games. On the days when she was not allowed out (of which there were many) she would announce: "Let's play Hunt the Minotaur."

"Oh, lord! Why can't we play Halma, or dominoes, or Racing Demon?"

I was rather lazy, and would always prefer to sit still and play a card game or a board game. To me, they had more point than her endless pretences. But Becky, who spent hours in bed reading when she had bronchitis, produced a nonstop flow of ideas gathered from books.

The house was full of big, old-fashioned screens, vitally necessary to keep draughts at bay. (Remember that this was before the days of central heating; coal and wood fires were all we had to warm us.) Becky fetched all the screens into Uncle Simon's study and constructed a maze with narrow passages between the folding walls.

"You can be Theseus and I'll be Ariadne – but what can we do for a Minotaur?"

"What is a Minotaur?" I would ask glumly, longing to get away and play Clock Patience or read *Lives of the Hunted*. I cared little for all the story-books they had in that house; but luckily they also had a good number of animal books, which, though not as interesting as books about aircraft or cars, were better than nothing.

"A Minotaur is a frightful monster, half man, half bull, which eats a person every day and lives in a maze. I think we'll just have to *imagine* the Minotaur."

"All right," I would agree, yawning, longing for the game to be over.

When we could go out, things were not so bad – except for the afternoons when Aunt Nesta asked us to push the little boys in their pushchairs down into the town on some shopping errand. Those were dreadful excursions. I felt such a fool, acting as nursery-maid to little Robbie or little Will. Not that they misbehaved, but I was sure, all the time we were out, that people were laughing or sneering at us (though they concealed it), and I loathed the old ladies who hung over the brats, cooing and chirruping.

"Eh, how they do grow! Eh, the bonnie wee mannie!"

Becky didn't seem to mind; she knew all the old ladies, of course. Even worse, they all seemed to know *me* although I couldn't tell one from another.

"Weel, weel, John, boy, it's grand to have ye back again. Ach, yer mither ought to let ye stop here a' the year round, she ought indeed." The very thought made me shiver with horror.

I had a useful trick for keeping the little boys quiet and quelled, which had also worked excellently on Becky when we were both younger and I wanted to get my own way if we disagreed about something. I had this knack of *shaking my eyes*. I am the only person I have ever come across with this ability, and I have long ago forgotten when or how I discovered the skill: I simply let both eyes go out of focus and blur, until they started to vibrate from side to side, which they did very fast – about as fast as a woodpecker working on a tree. It was quite a strain to keep it up for more than a minute, but seemed to do the eyes no harm; for all I know it may be good exercise for the muscles, or relax the optic nerve.

Anyway, for a number of years it gave me complete control over Becky. I can't think – or couldn't think then – why it should be frightening, but quite plainly it *was* so. She used to weep with sheer terror, and beg me to stop.

"Oh, please don't do it, John – *please* don't. You look

awful!" (Annoyingly, I could not, myself, see how I looked.
I tried to study myself in a mirror when alone, but my vision,
of course, blurred while my eyes were oscillating and all I
could see was a vague shape in the glass. That was then.
Now, I know more.) "It's so – it makes you look not *human*!
As if some horrible, evil creature had got into your body.
Please, *please* stop. We'll play draughts if that's what you'd
rather – you can have the book, I'll find something else to
read – we'll listen to cricket on the radio instead of going out
– I'll ask Mummy if we can have tomato soup for
supper . . ."

It was a first-rate way of getting what I wanted.

And then, one year, I suddenly found that it had lost its
power; even if I pulled a horrible face while I made my eyes
quiver – bared my teeth, glared, snarled – she simply
laughed her mild, comfortable laugh (my cousin Becky had
no sense of humour whatever) and said indulgently, "Oh,
John, you *are* funny when you do that!"

But the trick still worked well with the little boys.

Can I do it still? I haven't tried for thirty years. And have
no intention of doing so. Not after what happened . . .

But that comes later in the story.

At least when we were out in the street, therefore, the
boys were humble and biddable; though at home they could
sometimes be perfect little devils. Luckily my Aunt Nesta
had a young girl from the town who came and took them out
on most afternoons. And then Becky and I could climb trees
or get up on top of the garden wall (I showed her how, she

would never have dared to do it on her own) or, if the weather was not snowy, we could go up on the moor behind the house. This was interesting because it still had trenches dug for Civil Defence in the last war. They were like tunnels with the heather growing across the top. Becky didn't like them much, unless she was allowed to play Saxons and Normans, or Romans and Picts – one or another of her silly pretend games.

Oh, how bored I used to get on those visits to Marwick! And the worst part of all was Christmas itself. Aunt Nesta and Uncle Simon did not go in for a great deal of Christmas ritual and tradition. They were plain, simple people. He drove off each day to his job at the steelworks, she house-kept and looked after the children and saw that Becky's chest was well wrapped up. They could not afford and did not wish for expensive entertainments or fancy habits. At Christmas dinner they always asked in some old person from the town who would otherwise have been alone; they had a small Christmas tree, simply decorated with gilded pinecones and nuts and red paper flowers; and a rather modest quantity of brandy was poured over the pudding. "Christmas should be in the heart," Aunt Nesta would say, "not in a lot of fancy extras."

But in one way – I suppose, in the way that counted – they did take trouble and spend money. And that was over presents.

My presents from my parents were always exactly the same. From my father, his latest textbook. *Architecture for*

Sixth Forms; *Cellular Structure Explained*; *Optics Made Easy*; *Understanding the Differential Calculus*; *The Principles of Physics*; *A Comprehensive View of Modern History*; *Basic Geography*; *Space Made Simple* – there never was a subject that my father was not prepared to tackle. I had a whole row of his books standing on my bedroom mantelpiece at home, some in fancy leather bindings made up by the publisher as a commemorative gift to my father on their twentieth reprinting. His books sold for ever. All he needed to do was revise them from time to time.

My mother invariably gave me two new shirts.

These presents were always packed in my bag when I left for Marwick, wrapped in red Christmas paper, ready for me to open them on Christmas day. Often I left them unopened and brought them home still wrapped, unless I happened to have used all my shirts and needed another.

Christmas would have been bleak indeed if their gifts were all I had to rely on. But Uncle Simon and Aunt Nesta did not stop at just one present; they gave a whole series: books, comfortable casual clothes, chocolates, games, toys, or, simply, interesting *things*. Once Uncle Simon gave me a powder horn, studded with coral and turquoise beads. Once a snake, beaded all over and along its side the message: MADE BY TURKISH PRISONERS OF WAR 1918. Then there was a tiny Indian brass box . . .

And was I grateful for this largesse? No, I was not. I was very ungrateful, as you shall hear.

Every year, besides the fudge, mittens, books, diary, pocket-torch, cap-pistol, or whatever, there would be one superior present: the *main present*, Becky used to call it. And their habit over this was to give the same thing to each of us. One year, a fine case of pastel crayons. One year, really handsome paintboxes. One year it was a microscope; not a full-sized one, but not a toy; a real microscope, with slides, and lenses of varying power, and small specimen boxes and tweezers and pins; the sort of thing that anybody would be proud to have on their bedroom table. Another year it was a telescope. And, yet another time, a small but functioning easel, and a set of oil paints, turpentine, linseed oil, brushes, and palette.

Yet, I am sorry to say, these "main presents" called out my anger, envy, and hostility more than anything else. Why? Because of the difference in scale between Becky's and mine. If we had boxes of pastels – beautiful, high-quality pastels, nestling in corrugated slots, encased in elegant olive-wood boxes – Becky's box would have fifty crayons in it, mine only forty. Her paintbox, her microscope, her easel would always be a size larger than the one chosen for me. Not a great deal larger, but . . .

"Why did they give you a bigger one? It's not fair!" I blurted angrily to Becky on the first occasion – the paintboxes, perhaps.

Becky wrinkled her fair brows; to her it seemed simple, fair, and reasonable.

"Well, first, I'm a year older than you. So I *should* have a bigger present. And, second, I *am* their daughter; you are only a visitor. You come only once a year."

At any other moment I would have thought, And thank goodness for that! But now I felt bitterly resentful. After all, in other ways they treated me as one of the family; why not equal status in this?

"Because you are a year younger," Becky kept repeating. "It wouldn't be proper to give you exactly the same size as me."

And she looked at me with what seemed to me infuriating smugness. It always annoyed me when she referred to that year's difference, for I was decidedly the taller and stronger, and, besides, knew a great deal more about trains, aircraft, cars, machinery, and mathematics. The only area in which Becky came out on top was her skill at drawing pictures or painting – she was very good at that – and, of course, her tiresome inventiveness when it came to making up stories.

And to do her justice, she never once said, "After all, you weren't even invited here in the first place. Your parents asked mine if you could come."

One Christmas – the one that I remember most painfully and the memory of which has, ever since, given me a nervous dread of finding myself alone at that time – Becky received an extra present besides her "main" one.

The extra present was from her godfather in America. He was known as Uncle Joe, though not really related – he was Lord Gaystreet and had once been Aunt Nesta's Head of Department when she worked in an Embassy. He often forgot to send presents for several years, but when they did come they were memorable. Once it was a dolls' house; a complete replica of an Italian palace, with furniture to match. Once a gold-painted pedal car (he had forgotten, just then, that Becky was not a boy). I'd always longed for a pedal-car when I was younger (of course my parents would not think of giving me such an article) and was bitterly jealous of a gift that Becky never cared for – though the little boys loved it, of course. Later Uncle Joe sent her a bike with every possible gear and gadget, which I rode much more than she did. Then roller-skates, transistors, cameras . . . I was jealous, not only of the presents, but the fact that she should have a godfather who was a Lord. What had she ever done to deserve such luck?

On the year I am recalling, the wooden box from him was large and, as usual, covered with foreign stamps and customs labels. On Christmas morning, Becky left it until all the other presents had been opened.

Inside the wooden box was a cardboard one; inside that, a lot of wood-shavings; under the shavings, a layer of what felt like sheep's wool. Inside that, purple crinkly paper. At last she extracted two objects – large dolls.

But what dolls! Even I, who had always despised dolls, found them impressive. First, their size: each of them was about as high as my leg to the knee. One was male, one female. He had black moustaches, a sword and a pistol, she had long glossy black hair, layers and layers of silk petti-coats, and a fan which opened. Their black eyes opened, shut, and rolled. Their clothes were hand-made and splendid. "*Real* satin skirts, *real* velvet breeches," breathed Aunt Nesta, awed, inspecting them. "I wonder what country they are from? Eastern European, perhaps – or Turkish, or Russian."

"Russian seems likely," put in Uncle Simon. "Look, they are wearing skates."

Becky, meanwhile, delving into the bottom of the box, found several sets of different clothes, and also a small box which proved to contain batteries.

"Batteries! So they must be able to move!" cried Becky. She found slots in their backs, cunningly concealed under a velvet waistcoat, a silk shawl. She fitted the batteries into the slots.

Immediately the dolls became animated, fidgeted in her hands, and, when she put them down, tried to move about, but tripped over the Turkey rug.

"Take them into the passage!" cried the little boys.

On the slippery linoleum of the passage, or on the polished boards of the large, bare dining-room, the dolls skated with terrific proficiency, gliding, bowing, waltzing, reversing, pirouetting; it seemed almost impossible to believe that they were not small-scale humans. While in motion they kept almost within touching distance of one another. "They must be magnetized," said Uncle Simon.

Only when Becky grabbed them and removed the batteries did they stop skating.

She was in ecstasy over them, flushed and bright-eyed.

"I love them!" she said. "Uncle Joe never sent a better present. They are the best of all."

"There may be a little problem when the batteries run out," remarked Uncle Simon. "You won't be able to replace *those* in a hurry."

"When I write my thank-you letter to Uncle Joe I shall ask him if he can get some more."

"What shall you call them?" asked Aunt Nesta, beginning to tidy up wrapping paper and coloured ribbon.

Becky had no hesitation at all. "I shall call them Crespian and Clairan."

"Where on earth did you find *those* names?"

"In a map somewhere, I think," said Becky vaguely. "They seem just right."

It was a fiercely cold Christmas that year: not snowy, but with bitter winds plucking and keening, ice everywhere, the ground hard as a brick. Aunt Nesta was insistent on keeping Becky indoors. Becky was happy just to sit watching Crespian and Clairan perform their skilful, mysterious dance. On and on and on . . .

And I?

You'd think a boy of my age would not be interested in a pair of dolls. But, from the first moment I saw them, I was fascinated – hypnotised – bewitched. I coveted them. I longed, I burned for them.

Without the slightest hesitation, I set about planning how I would steal them from Becky.

I had often stolen smaller treasures from her. Small,

precious possessions that might – that *could* – get mislaid. Ivory elephants. The little brass box – it had, in fact, been hers; I hid it inside my sponge-bag when I returned home, and if she suspected that I had made off with it, she never accused me. And likewise with the grandfather clock from the dolls' house (which really told the time), with a signet-ring, a silver penknife, a gold pen, and other articles. I felt, simply, that I had a *right* to them; why should they remain in Becky's ownership when *I* wanted them? At home, my parents never inquired how I came into possession of these things – very likely they never even noticed, since they took no interest in me or my belongings.

But the dolls were so large, extraordinary, and conspicuous that I would have to take some pains to conceal their presence when I got home, and only let them perform when my mother and father were out of the house – which they were, luckily, a good deal of the time. And my bedroom floor was polished pine; that would make a good skating rink . . .

But, of course, the main problem was going to be stealing them from Becky in such a way that neither she nor Uncle Simon nor Aunt Nesta could possibly suspect me. As a matter of fact it did not take me long to come up with what seemed a cast-iron plan.

On Boxing Day afternoon Uncle Simon and Aunt Nesta took the little boys off to a small-children's party. Becky and I were too old to be invited and, though we had suggested taking a walk on the moor, Aunt Nesta decided that it was too cold.

"The wind is too bitter for you, my honey. Stay indoors read some of your new books, paint a picture with your oilpaints, play with Crespian and Clairan. Such names!" she went on, laughing. "But they seem suitable, I must say."

Off went the family. And I, meantime, by continual quiet repetition, had persuaded Becky that it would be a wicked shame, a shocking waste, an almost criminal loss of opportunity, if we did not try out the skating dolls on *real ice*. Which, of course, was there, ready to hand, at the bottom of the garden.

"Dad doesn't like us going near the pond unless he's there," she said doubtfully.

"It must be frozen really thick by now," I argued. "And *we* don't have to go on it – only the dolls. We can always get them back with a rake if they go too far from the edge."

Of course she was beguiled by the idea. I played on her guilt, too.

"*You've* got a rich godfather who sends you fancy presents. I never get anything like that. So it's only fair that we should try out my idea."

At last she agreed; and while she was putting on an extra pair of stockings, a chest-protector, flannel petticoat, a second sweater, I slipped outside and prepared for my plan by hacking a good-sized hole in the ice with a pickaxe, borrowed from the garden shed when I fetched the rake.

Then I went back to the house.

"*Aren't you ready yet?*"

"Just coming," she said, tying the second shoelace. "And I must put on my hood."

"I'll carry the dolls out," I said. "I'll be slotting in the batteries."

"All right," she said, "but don't put them on the ice till I come—"

"Hey, listen!" I said. "I think that's the phone. You'd better answer – it might be your granny."

Becky did not stop to consider how unlikely this was – Uncle Simon's mother had already rung up that morning – but hurried off to the little bare telephone room. And I hared down to the garden shed, where I hid the two dolls in a nest of hessian, already prepared for them.

By the time that Becky reached the pond, there was nothing to be seen but a hole through the ice, in which, with the rake, I was frantically fishing and dredging.

"Oh, no!" cried Becky in horror, and before I could stop her she ran out on to the cracked surface of the pond . . .

I still hate to think about the next few hours. Naturally, in planning to steal the dolls from my cousin Becky, I had never intended that she should suffer a ducking in sub-zero water and come down with pneumonia.

I was packed off home, of course; first, because of my disgraceful behaviour, second, because everybody was far too busy nursing Becky to want me about the place. I was just a horrible reminder of what shouldn't have happened.

Since Mother and Father were fixed for another month in their villa, and could not for a moment consider such a jolt in their programme as a premature return home to take care of me, my Aunt Joscelyn was summoned from Bromley and came, very much put out, to stay in our house.

She was there when I arrived, not to welcome but to denounce.

"A fine trick to play on your poor cousin! A nice, stupid piece of behaviour. Causing all this upset! Well, don't just stand gawping – take your bag upstairs and unpack."

Of course I was dying to do just that. In all the turmoil at Kelso House nobody had thought to inquire about the dolls; they were still in my possession.

I scuttled up to my room and opened my suitcase. The dolls were still wrapped in hessian, as I had furtively thrust them under a pile of shirts. I took them out, fitted in the batteries – and received a freezing, breath-stopping shock . . .

My Aunt Joscelyn was a brisk, bossy, interfering woman, quite unlike my parents. They never bothered to set foot in my room, but she had followed me up the stairs, calling out some instructions about dirty clothes. I just had time to fling a dressing-gown over the bodies of the dolls before she strode into the room.

"Just as I expected – clean and dirty things all mixed up. What's the matter? You look absolutely green!"

"I feel a bit sick," I had the presence of mind to mumble.

"That'll be the long journey. You'd best go straight to bed. Here – I'll fetch the dirty-clothes basket, and all this stuff can go straight in it."

While she was doing that, I thrust Clairan and Crespian under the bed, keeping my eyes screwed tight shut while I removed the batteries. . . .

After a day or two, Joscelyn said: "What in the world's the matter with you, boy? You're pale as a dish-rag and nervous as a cricket. When I tapped you on the shoulder just now, you jumped six inches in the air. Don't tell me it's because of your cousin Becky; you weren't *that* fond of her?"

"It's nothing," I muttered. "I just don't feel very well."

"It'll be a good thing when school starts again. You spend far too much time up in that room of yours, moping."

I spent almost *all* my time up there, staring at the dolls. I did not want to; I did not intend to; and yet, day after miserable day, I found myself obeying the irresistible urge to go up there, fetch them out from under the bed, take the batteries from the box, slot them in, and then watch, hypnotised, sick with terror, while Crespian and Clairan gazed back at me.

At night I dreamed about them, staring, staring. At other times I thought about them, lying there under the bed, with their eyes waiting for me.

A good way to escape – the only way – would be to run down the stairs, down the street, and throw myself into the icy river . . .

I became less and less responsive or aware of other people – sounds, voices, footsteps, remarks made to me. The dolls were all I thought about. So, after about ten days when, one afternoon Joscelyn burst open my bedroom door, she found me crouched on the floor, staring at Crespian and Clairan, who were staring back at me. They did not skate any more. No, no.

"I've some bad news – your cousin Becky has died—" Joscelyn began. And then her voice gave out, her eyes were fixed, glued, on the dolls. "Merciful heavens!" she whispered. "What in the world are those horrible things? And *why do they shake their eyes from side to side like that?*"

All the eyes – hers and theirs – swam together in a dizzy circle, and I fainted.

When I came to, my Aunt Joscelyn told me sternly that the dolls had been burned in the garden incinerator. "The best place for them, if you ask me. And now you had better tell me the whole story," she said.

So I told it to her, as I have told it to you.

I never went back to Marwick.

And that is why (the headmaster said) I run a school for delinquents. I know such a lot about stealing.

ACROSS THE FIELDS

Susan Price

 brazier held the fire in the centre of the hut. Its iron bars were crumbling with rust but the coals were red-hot inside, sending out waves of heat to meet the long thin draughts of cold wind that came in through the gaps in the planking walls. The men, their bodies blackened with a coating of sweat, water and coal-dust, crowded close to the fire, shivering and trying to wipe themselves dry with old rags, shirts or sheets of newspaper.

"Never mind – Christmas tomorrow!" one of them shouted, and the others laughed. Christmas Day was the only day in the whole year the mine didn't work.

When they were more or less dry, though still filthy with coal-dust, the men pulled on trousers, shirts and jackets. In 1924, there were no pit-head baths. They crowded around the fire, shoulders jostling, trying to get warm before the long, dark walk home. From hand to hand passed the jug of beer the mine-owner left in the hut for every shift of men coming up the shaft. As they drank, or waited for their turn to drink, they listened to the wind blowing around the hut and shrieking in the gaps.

"Our Grace'll be walking tonight," one of the men said, and there was more laughter.

There was a soft rap on the door of the hut, which only the nearest man heard. He opened it a crack, and then pulled it wide to allow someone to come in.

"Jon!" he called. "Tha little sister here, come to walk home with thee, so thee don't get scared!"

That made all the men laugh again, and several of them began coughing badly. The girl recognised her brother's cough among them, sharp and loud. Jon almost always coughed when other people laughed.

The men crowded together to let the girl come to the fire and stand beside her brother. She was about thirteen, tall for her age and thin, wearing a long, limp skirt that almost hid her boots. On her head was a man's old cap, with a thick tartan shawl folded over it and wrapped tightly about her body. Between the cap's peak and the shawl her eyes glistened brightly, and her nose glowed a bright red from the cold outside.

She looked quickly and shyly at all the men's faces. Even though she was standing beside him, she wasn't quite sure that she recognised her brother. All the faces were black and shiny, as if they'd been polished with the black lead that her mother used on the cooking-range at home; and in the tawny, golden-red light from the fire, their faces shone gilded, as the range shone by the light of the fire. But their eyes glittered white, and every glance and swivel of their eyeballs seemed exaggerated and comic and horrible all at once. And their lips, washed by the beer, were bright red.

With a final cough, the man beside her said, "What's up, Emily?" Then she knew for sure it was Jon.

"Have tha been paid?" she asked, and jumped as all the men around her laughed aloud.

"After thy money! Her's learning early!" one said.

"I shall be paid tonight," Jon replied.

"Mother wants thee to fetch the meat for our Christmas dinner."

Jon nodded, and took the jug from the man beside him. As he drank, the other miner asked the girl, "Thee walk here on thy own, me flower? In the dark?"

She nodded.

"And tha weren't scared?" he asked. He grinned at her.

From the other side of the brazier, another man said, "Did tha meet Our Grace?"

"Ar, with her dead white face and her long wet hair hanging down her back," said another, "and her eyes staring, and her hands reaching out for whoever her can find—"

The miners laughed as the girl turned aside from them, pretending she wasn't interested. She knew who they were talking about: everyone in the neighbourhood knew the story of Grace, the gypsy girl who had drowned herself in the flooded clay-pit and now, so people said, walked over the fields at night, trying to find and drown others.

"Jon, hurry up," Emily said. "We've got to get that meat."

"Plenty of time," Jon said. It was true. The market would stay open until at least nine, and it could only be about seven now.

"Her don't want to be out late," said a miner, and nudged Jon. "If tha'm out late, tha might meet Padfoot." He stooped towards Emily. "Tha sure tha didn't hear Padfoot padding along after thee as tha come along that path?"

"I don't believe in ghosts," Emily said, and the hut was filled again with the row of the miners' laughter.

"Hey, be serious, though," said another miner.

"Have thee ever heard that screaming as tha was walking home?" asked a third man. "I remember the time—"

Emily moved close to Jon and looked pleadingly up at him. She didn't want to hear any more of these frightening stories. Jon smiled his red-lipped smile and shouted, "Happy Christmas, lads! We'm going."

He reached out and opened the door of the hut, letting in a broad, cold blast of air as he and Emily moved out into the darkness, followed by a cheery, beery chorus of, "Happy Christmas! Happy Christmas, little un! Happy Christmas!"

Outside in the dark, another fire burned near the mine-shaft, an open, brick-lined hole in the ground. It was the only light to be seen nearby; beyond its flickering was deep darkness. Jon passed by the fire with his quick, long stride, and Emily hurried after him, her boots clop-clopping on the stony, hard-frozen ground. Above them glittered a wide expanse of silver stars.

A black shape loomed up ahead – it was the mine office. They rounded the building, and Emily was glad to see yellow lamplight spilling from its windows. She waited outside, leaning against the wooden wall and hugging herself inside her shawl, while Jon went in to hand over his candle-can and collect his money. Emily was cold and wished he would hurry up. Even there, in the mine yard, she didn't like the dark. She couldn't help thinking that Our Grace might suddenly whip into sight, with her long wet hair, her white drowned face and her reaching hands. Even the knowledge that Jon and the light of the mine office were only a step behind her didn't make her feel any better. She would still have *seen* Grace – her swollen drowned face and her mouth moving as she called your name.

Quickly Emily pushed the door and went into the office, to stand close behind Jon, so close that she touched him. Being near her brother always made her feel better. He never seemed to be afraid of anything: not of going underground, nor of the dark, or big dogs, or strangers, or mice or spiders or anything. Yet still she looked fearfully towards the door, wondering if the yellow light of the oil lamp would really keep Grace out of the office if she were in the yard.

Jon felt her touch against him, looked down and smiled. "Come on, Chuck," he said, moving towards the door. She followed him. It meant going out into the dark again, but at least now she would be with Jon, and she didn't fear ghosts as much while he was with her. He walked to work in the dark most days, he worked all day in the dark and walked home again in the dark, and he thought nothing of it. Ghosts didn't come near people who didn't believe in them, did they? So Emily hoped.

Jon had worked hard all day, but he still walked fast as he led the way, by dark, unlit field-paths, towards the town of Oldbury and its market. Emily had to put many a hop and skip in her walk to stop herself from falling behind. Slipping one hand out of her shawl, she gripped him by the belt to help herself.

"Here," he said. "Keep thy hand warm." And he slipped her arm through his, and held her hand in his dirty warm one. His hands were always hot, as if he had a fire burning in him. But she was still out of breath by the time they reached Oldbury.

The market place was lit by flaring white gas lamps with pitch black shadows between pools of light. There were still many people about: all those who had delayed shopping for their Christmas dinner as long as possible in order to buy cheap. Jon and Emily kept their arms linked as they pushed through the crowds and made their way to the butcher's stalls, where blood had collected in pools between the cobbles, and where chickens' heads and legs lay scattered everywhere. Even in the cold, there was a bad smell of blood and flesh and chickens' guts.

Jon was tired and wanted to get home, bath and sleep, so he didn't take long about marketing. On one stall he spotted a large goose hanging by its legs.

"I bet," he said to Emily, "that he can't sell that. Too big. Nobody wants it. How much for the big 'un, mate?" he called to the stallholder, pointing to the goose.

The stallholder looked up at the bird and pulled a face. He knew that he wasn't going to sell the bird, and he had no way of keeping it fresh to sell another day. "Seven and six," he said.

"I'll give thee five shilling," Jon said, and the stallholder took the bird down without another word, and began wrapping it in newspaper.

Emily wasn't happy. "Too much!" she whispered.

"It's Christmas," Jon said, and went on to buy sweets for her and for the two other sisters and three brothers at home.

"We'll have no money *left*," Emily said, wanting the sweets, but afraid of what their mother would say.

"It's my money," said Jon.

They started walking home, Jon's pockets stuffed with bags of sweets, and his arms wrapped round the goose. Emily held on to his belt to help her keep up, her hand warmed by the shelter of his jacket and the heat of his body through his shirt. She was tired, having been up early to scrub the kitchen floor before going to school, then running errands after school and finally coming on this long walk with her brother. She leaned her head on his arm as they walked.

Once they were out of town, they were faced with a long, long road home. Jon suddenly stopped walking, hugging the goose to himself and lowering his head. Emily knew that he was overcome with the thought of how far they had yet to walk before they were home. And then he still had to bath before he could go to bed. "It'd be shorter," he said, "if we cut across the fields."

Emily straightened up, lifting her head from his arm. She didn't like the idea at all. The fields were wide, cold, empty and dark. But she had to give a more sensible reason than that. "It's dangerous," she said. "What about all the old pit-workings and quarries? We might fall in one."

"I'm not walking all the way round," Jon said, turning off the road and striking out across the rough ground of the field.

Emily let go of his belt and stood for a moment. She thought about walking home by herself. She looked about, up and down the road, but there was no one in sight, and the roadway, lit only by widely spaced gas lamps, seemed darker without Jon. And Jon, with his quick, long stride, and without her hanging on his belt, was already growing smaller, fading into the darkness. Even walking across the fields, she quickly decided, was better than walking all that way by herself, thinking about drowned Grace, and the ghost dog, Padfoot, whom you saw when you were going to die.

"Wait for me, Jon!" Hugging her shawl about her, Emily ran from the road over the field. The frozen ground was just as hard underfoot as the pavement, and frozen leaves rustled under her boots. Jon stopped and turned, waiting for her. Breathless, she caught up with him and wrapped her fingers about his belt again, under his jacket.

"We'll soon be home," he said. "Have a mincepie afore we go to bed."

They didn't waste breath on talking after that. Emily was surprised, as always, that Jon could walk so quickly after spending all day crouching underground, hacking at rock and coal. He swung on, stride after quick stride, hugging the dead goose to his chest, his head lowered to watch where he put his feet, his breath drifting before him in puff after puff of white mist. Emily's own breath wreathed her face as she panted beside him, forced to work her legs just a little too fast, so that her hips ached. Her heels jolted hard on the ground and shook her with every step. Her throat was raw from gasping at the freezing air, but she didn't ask Jon to slow down. After all, she thought, peering around them into the dark, the quicker they walked, the sooner they would be home and safe from the night.

The fields around them could only be felt as a cold open space, over which the wind blew to scrape at them. Nothing could be seen but blackness; even the path beneath their feet was only a dimmer grey in the darkness. Emily hoped they were on the right path: in the dark, it could be any path.

251

And anything could be out there, in the darkness, hidden from them.

As they walked, Emily kept looking all round, glancing back over her shoulder every few seconds, and squinting her eyes to peer into the darkness ahead. If there was any danger, she wanted to see it before it reached them. But despite this care, she didn't see the man coming. She only heard his voice, suddenly barking out in the darkness on Jon's other side. "Evenin'."

Emily leaned around Jon and saw a stranger walking beside her brother. In the dark, she could just make out the darker area of his working clothes and the pale white stripe of his muffler. Between the muffler and the dark cap was the not-so-pale blur of his face.

"Evenin'," Jon said, friendly and unafraid, while Emily clung more tightly to his belt and pressed closer to him. The man was not the ghost she had feared, but now she was afraid that he was a robber or a murderer, who'd been waiting for them on this dark field path. "Happy Christmas," her brother added.

"Oh," said the man, his deep voice grumbling through the dark, cold air. "It ain't Christmas yet. Not 'til the last stroke of midnight."

Their feet crunched on the frost-hardened path – Jon's light, quick, steady tread and Emily's skip, hop and jump. She listened, but the stranger's feet made no sound.

The stranger spoke again: "Where thee going?"

"Home," Jon said. "As quick as we can."

"What's thy hurry?" asked the stranger. "Why don't tha come to the match? Tha could win a prize, strong lad like thee."

"Match?" Jon asked, and Emily tugged at his belt and whispered, "Jon!" But he either didn't hear her or took no notice.

"Wrestling match," said the stranger. "I know thee for a good wrestler, lad."

"Jon, we've got to get home," Emily said.

"There's prizes?" Jon asked. Their family always needed money or extra food, especially at Christmas. Whether the prize was money or a cake or another goose, it tempted Jon.

"There's prizes," said the stranger, and Emily didn't like the way he said it – as if there were other things he wasn't saying.

"A bout or two then," Jon said, not seeming to notice anything odd about the way the man had spoken. Emily tugged at his belt but he ignored her, and she could have wept with anger and disappointment. She so much wanted to get home and safely into the warmth and light.

"Oh Jon, let's go home," she wailed. "Tha'm tired. Come home, go to bed."

Jon looked round. "Thee run on home," he said, sounding bad-tempered.

Emily looked ahead at the thin path of hard dirt that ran through long, grey tussocks of wilted, frozen grass and leafless bushes, and quickly faded into black winter darkness. She almost did as he said: she could see herself, in her imagination, running hard along the path until she reached the safety of streets and houses. In imagination, she could feel her running feet hitting the ground.

But she was afraid of what she might meet on her own, without Jon's warmth and confidence to keep the ghosts away. And she was afraid to leave her brother alone too, without her fears to warn him, trusting and friendly as he was. As he protected her, so, she felt, she protected him: they should stay together. Who knew who this stranger was, or what he really wanted? He might kill Jon to get the goose.

"I'll come with thee," she said, in a small, frightened voice.

She imagined the man taking something heavy from his pocket, like a brick or an iron bar, and hitting Jon on the head with it, and she knew she couldn't stop him, but she also felt, fiercely, that she could try. She could kick the man hard; she could bite him till he bled. She could shout and shout, louder than she'd ever shouted; she could run and fetch help. Even if she couldn't stop the man hurting Jon, she could make sure he didn't get away with it.

The stranger left the path and struck off through the long, crunching, frozen grass of the field. Jon followed him and Emily, clutching at Jon's belt, followed Jon. Whenever she could, Emily peered around Jon at the stranger, trying to see what he looked like so that she could describe him to the police if she had to. But she could never see his face clearly. It was always hidden by his cap, or by his turned-up collar and muffler. She thought he had a dark moustache; she thought his cheeks and chin were darkened by beard-stubble; but that was as much as she could tell.

Just you try anything, she thought at him. Just you try. I'll kick your feet from under you. I'll bite your fingers off. I'll – she wished very much that she was bigger and stronger.

They were very far from the path now, and when Emily looked around and behind them, she saw nothing but deep, blue-grey darkness, with black shapes of low bushes emerging from it. But from ahead came a noise. It was a murmur, buzzing and rising and falling: the sound of voices clamouring together as they had clamoured in the market-place – but here the sound had a colder, more frozen note as it faded and was lost in the open fields. She wanted to ask Jon, one more time, not to go to this meeting, but to come home with her – but she knew that he wouldn't change his mind now.

There was light ahead: red and golden light, shining out of the darkness like a jewel. Black shapes moved across it, blocking out its light and then letting it shine again – a fire with people moving around it. Jon picked up his heels and walked even more quickly, to reach the fire and the people, and Emily had to run to stay with him. She felt tears in her eyes as she ran towards what frightened her.

They came nearer to the fire, and felt its heat blow towards them on the wind, bringing a shower of sparks and cinders together with an ashy smell of burning. The stranger began to clap his hands and shout, "Here we be, here we be! Here's a lad to give we a bout! Here's a lad who'll bet his wages, his goose, and his heart and soul!"

Emily didn't like the sound of that; and she didn't like it when the people left the fire and came to meet them, crowding around them so that they were hemmed in. She didn't like it when men pressed close and began to slap Jon on the shoulders, because she was so small among them that she felt she was being smothered in the crowd, and because she was afraid she would lose her grip on Jon's belt and be pushed away from him. She took hold of his belt with both hands, and let herself be dragged almost off her feet as he was carried forward in the noise of the crowd, closer to the light and heat of the fire.

A dark young man, as tall as Jon but broader, stood squarely between them and the fire. His face was in deep shadow and couldn't be seen. He started to take off his jacket, and as he did so, he said, "For the goose."

Jon grinned and passed the goose to Emily. She took it, soft, limp and heavy, in her arms. Jon took off his cap and put it on Emily's head, on top of the shawl and cap she already wore. He unwound his muffler and hung it around her neck; and he took off his jacket and draped it around her shoulders. Then, in his shirt-sleeves, in the bitter cold, he bent at the knees and held his arms out to the other young man. The crowd around them backed away to give them room.

Emily hated being there and having to watch. She felt desperately that Jon must win – felt it so much that it hurt – not only because he was her brother but because if he lost the goose, the whole family would have to go without Christmas dinner, and the five shillings spent on it would be wasted. She didn't think they would dare go home and face her mother after spending five shillings on a goose and then losing it.

And wrestling was a rough game. The other man looked heavier than Jon. If he was a better wrestler as well, then Jon could be badly hurt, and if Jon was hurt, then he wouldn't be able to work, and they were always short of money even when Jon was in work. Jon had to win, he *had* to, he *had* to! She hugged the goose tightly, and swallowed over a painful, hot lump in her throat.

The two men had wrapped their arms around each other, and were now trying to crush the breath from each other's ribs while struggling to trip each other with their feet. Emily watched, her unblinking eyes watering in the cold, wishing hard for Jon to win. But the fear that he would lose was equal to all her hope. It was unbearable – unbearable to hope and fear so much, and she had to turn away from the wrestlers.

She found herself looking instead at the faces in the crowd, lit warmly red and gold by the light of the fire. And her eyes picked out one woman's face. She had seen that woman somewhere before—

She jumped as a shout went up all around her, shaking the

cold air. Jon was on the ground. The other had thrown him down. As she watched her brother got up and again they wrapped their arms around each other.

Emily looked again for the woman in the crowd. She couldn't see her any more, but she noticed a man. She knew his face too, but couldn't think of his name . . .

There was another shout, and Jon was on the ground again. Jon was losing! Oh, Jon! she thought, hugging their goose, their Christmas dinner, which they were going to lose: how could thee win when thee were so tired? Why didn't thee come home with me?

She had to look away again. She couldn't bear to watch. And there was another face she knew: the face of a boy this time. Now she knew that boy's face very well. Who was he . . .?

The crowd shouted a third time, but Emily didn't look to see which of the wrestlers had been thrown. She remembered where she had seen the boy before. He had been in her class at school – had it been last year or the year before? But he was no longer at school because – she turned even colder as she remembered – because he had died. He had died of consumption. She had seen his funeral go past in the street. They had prayed for him at school, and had been asked to remember him. Dead and buried, that boy, yet here he was at this Christmas Eve wrestling match, out in the wild, dark fields.

She felt a tugging at the goose in her arms, and looked up into the face of the dark young man, Jon's opponent. He was taking the goose from her. "I won," he said. And he wasn't even out of breath.

Emily let him take the goose, because he had won it and because she was afraid. She remembered where she had seen the woman she had noticed earlier . . . That woman had lived three doors away from them when Emily had been a little girl, until she had gone away. It had been a long time before Emily discovered that the woman had died. And the man she had noticed . . . She had seen the man with Jon. Long ago, when Jon had first started working down the pit, he had worked with that man. Emily had seen him outside the pub, laughing and joking with Jon. And Jon had gone to his funeral after he had been killed by a roof-fall in the mine.

Shrinking in on herself, hugging herself small, she glanced quickly at the crowd about her, and thought: dead, all dead. We're in company with the dead.

Jon had got to his feet, and had come over to her and the young man who now held the goose.

"I wasn't ready," he said, breathing hard and short, out of breath. He coughed before adding. "Again. I'll win the goose back."

"Jon," Emily said, reaching out for him. "No." She wanted to tell him about the people around them. She wanted to point out the dead neighbour-woman and his dead workmate and her dead schoolfriend. But her voice squeaked like a mouse, and Jon took no notice of his nervous little sister.

"The goose if thou win," said the dark, dead young man. "What if I win?"

Jon reached into his trouser-pocket, and they heard the jingle of coins.

"I've no use for money," said the dark young man.

Jon dropped the coins back into his pocket and looked up in surprise. "What, then?"

Emily felt all the people around – all the dead people – move closer; and she darted to Jon and put her arms around his waist. He absentmindedly dropped his arm around her shoulders as he waited for an answer.

"Thy heart and soul," said the dark young man.

Emily hugged Jon tighter in warning, but Jon laughed and coughed, and said, "Me heart and soul? What use be them to thee?"

The fire flared and its red light glowed over the dark young man's face, showing the damp twist of his hair and the deep hollows above and below his eyes, the skin stretched tight over his cheekbones, and the shape of his teeth showing through his lips.

As Emily held on to Jon, she felt him start with shock. "Tom Rugeley!" he cried, drawing a long breath of cold air, which made him cough. Emily, hugging him, felt the coughs shake him. "Tha'm dead, Tom," Jon said. And then he said, to himself, "I'm dreaming."

"Bet me thy heart and soul," said Tom Rugeley. "I'll dance to the beat of thy heart – mine don't dance no more. I'll feel with thy soul – mine don't feel no more. If I win, I'll live in thee – and thou won't live no more."

Emily felt Jon's arm tighten around her, and his other arm come round her too. He lifted her right off her feet, up to his chest, and she felt him move a step or two. He was going to run and take her with him. But then he stopped, and looking about, Emily saw the people all around them coming closer, their arms held out to block their way. Jon's grip on her loosened, and she slipped back to the ground. There were too many of the dead, all around them and all too strong. They could not run away.

"Then we'll wrestle," Jon said, "but here's the wager. If I lose, me heart and soul. But if I win, the little wench goes home with the goose."

When she heard that, Emily's heart swelled and grew full and sore with love and gratitude. Tears pressed against the backs of her eyes, and she took Jon's warm hand in both of hers and held it tight.

All around them the dead murmured and whispered, and to the front of the crowd came pushing the dead women, the young girls, and the little girls who had died as children. They all stared at Emily with their sunken eyes and there was one – Emily shivered and hid her face against Jon's shirt-sleeve – there was one with long black hair hanging over her shoulders that dripped water on to the ground even in this freezing weather. A man's voice from the back of the crowd called, "Grace!" and she turned her head, that one, water flying from her hair. And the whispering, the murmuring from all the dead women and girls said, "But we want her. We want her . . ."

"Then it's a good wager!" Jon said. "More to win, more to lose! My heart and my soul against the little wench and the goose. What tha say, Tom?"

Tom Rugeley looked around at the dead, and then he looked back at Jon and slowly, despite the cold whispering in the air, he nodded.

Jon pushed Emily gently away from him and the second wrestling match began.

Emily watched this time, gritting her teeth until her jaws ached as Jon strained to throw the dead man and not be thrown himself. By sheer skill, he got his foot around the foot of the dead man, and threw him over his hip to the ground. But the dead man got up again at once – no struggle can tire nor fall hurt a dead man – and closed with Jon again. And Emily watched, her heart aching more each time, as her brother was thrown once, twice, three times, and lost the match.

How else could it have ended? Jon had worked all day, and walked to market and back, and fought one bout already, while his opponent would fight always with the same untiring strength. He had lost, and now he lay on the hard, frozen ground where he had been thrown, while all the dead turned to Emily.

"New lives for old," said Tom Rugeley. "Who shall I give the little wench to?"

"Thou hasn't won me!" Emily said. Her voice shrilled out through the dark, sharp with fright. "Jon lost, so tha've won him, heart and soul. But tha've not won me."

"Art going to wrestle?" asked Tom Rugeley, and around them came the dry laughter of the dead.

Emily ran across the little open space at the centre of the gathering, to where Jon half-sat, half-lay on the ground. She took his jacket from around her own shoulders and put it around his. "I can't wrestle," she said, "but I can riddle. I'll ask thee a riddle. If tha can answer it, thou shall ask me one. First one who can't answer is the loser."

"But what's the wager?" asked the dead man.

"If I lose, tha win us both," said Emily. "If I win, tha lose us both. Win all, lose all."

The dead crowded close; the dead whispered and shook their heads. But Emily said, "Fancy a dead man being scared to take a bet!"

"You're on!" said Tom Rugeley.

"And I'll ask the first riddle," she said. And she asked the hardest one she knew – one she had learned at school:

"In a hall as white as milk,
Lined with skin as soft as silk,
In a fountain crystal clear,
A golden apple does appear.
No doors there are to this stronghold,
But thieves break in and steal the gold.
What is it?"

"That's an old one," said Tom Rugeley, "and the answer's known to all of us here. It's an egg. And now I ask one. How many wild strawberries grow in the salt sea?"

Emily was kneeling on the ground beside Jon, and she looked into his face, hoping he might know the answer. She could hardly see his face in the dark, but even so it was plain that he had no more idea than she had. "How many wild strawberries . . .?" she said, and knew that the answer must be a tricky one.

And then it seemed to her that she had heard the riddle before, and knew the answer. She snatched at it without wondering what it meant – "As many as fish swim in the forest!" She saw by the way the dead people's shoulders sagged in disappointment that she had given the right answer.

"Here's my next riddle." It was another hard one she'd been taught at school:

"White bird featherless
Flew from Paradise,
Landed on the castle wall.
Along came Sir Landless
Took it up handless
Rode away horseless
To the King's white hall
What is it?"

"Another old riddle," said Tom Rugeley. "What's old we know. The answer is: a snowflake in the wind. Here's my riddle: How quickly can you travel round the world?"

This is hard, thought Emily. The dead man knew far better riddles than she did. She had no idea of how long it would take to travel even to Wales. But then the answer suddenly jumped into her head.

"If you get up with the sun, and keep up with the sun, you can travel all round in the world in one day – like the Sun does. And here's my riddle."

And, she thought, I had better make it a good one, a new one, because I might not be able to answer another one of his. She thought: make it a new one. The dead know all the old riddles. And she began to think frantically, while the ghosts waited. Hurry, hurry! she kept telling herself. Think of the answer first, then make a riddle to fit it. She thought so quickly that when she spoke the beginning of the riddle, she had no idea how it would end.

"I nothing fear but morning bird-song.
My heart is still, but still it longs.
By day I am gone, by night I show clear
Now riddle-me-ree-a
What be I?"

To her relief, Tom Rugeley didn't answer. He stared at her, and then looked around at the other dead. "A new riddle," he said.

"Can't thee answer it?" Emily asked. "Tha've lost if tha can't."

"I can answer it, I can answer it. 'By day I am gone, by night I show clear . . .'"

Emily and Jon sat together on the cold, hard ground, and

they looked at each other, and they waited. All around them the dead whispered together.

"Dost thee give up?" Emily asked. "Is it too hard?"

"Gone by day but clear by night," said Tom Rugeley, "It's the moon."

"No," Emily said.

"Then it's the stars," said another of the dead.

"No," Emily said.

The dead looked at each other. "Can't be the sun," one of them muttered.

"Dost give up?" Emily asked.

The night drew on, and it grew colder and colder. Emily and Jon sat wrapped in her thick, heavy shawl, huddling close together to keep warm amidst the cold company of the dead.

"'I nothing fear but morning bird-song,'" said Grace, the drowned girl whose hair never stopped dripping water. "Is it a worm?"

"No," said Emily, her head leaning on Jon's shoulder because she was so tired she couldn't hold up its weight.

"'My heart is still, but still it longs,'" said the dead man who had led them there. "I can't make owt of that."

"It's a stupid riddle!" said Tom Rugeley.

"Does that mean thee give up?" Emily asked.

"No!" And on and on went the guessing game, until midnight was passed, and then more hours, and there came the coldest, darkest time of the night, when Emily and Jon shivered together despite the shawl, and the deep cold set Jon coughing again.

The dead couldn't guess the answer to the riddle, but they wouldn't give up their chance of winning living hearts and souls either.

"It must be the moon! It can only be the moon!"

"No," Emily said, her eyes closed.

"Then it's the stars – has to be!"

"No."

"'My heart is still . . .' It must be something dead," said one of the ghosts thoughtfully, and Emily opened her eyes and held her breath. But the right answer didn't come.

But though they went on trying, the ghosts could not guess the answer. They went on trying until the sky was grey, and the air still colder than it had been all night. They went on trying until, from far over the field, came the first morning cock-call, the first cock-crow of Christmas Day. And on Christmas Day, and the twelve days of Christmas, ghosts and the dead and witches have no power.

As the cock crowed a second time, a rustle of movement ran through the crowd of dead. They drew back from Jon and Emily and looked at each other. And as the cock crowed a third time, they turned and ran away across the dark field. Without a sound they went: no shouting, and no sound of feet on the ground. They vanished into the deep grey of the morning twilight, running for their graves in all the little churchyards round about.

Jon and Emily knelt up on the hard, cold ground, and watched them go. Jon put his arms round Emily and hugged her tight.

They got to their feet, moving very stiffly and slowly because they were so cold. Jon picked up the goose and checked that his pockets were still full of sweets, and then they went on slowly across the fields to home.

They lived in a little house that was one in a long row. Jon lifted the latch and they went in. Their whole family was gathered in the little room. Mincepies were being made at the table: one sister was rolling out the pastry; a little brother was cutting the pastry out with a cup; another was greasing tins. Their mother was putting mincemeat into the cases. Everyone stopped what they were doing and looked up as they went in.

"Where have thee been?" their mother shouted.

Jon and Emily looked at each other.

"We come across the fields and we got lost," Jon said.

"I thought the bogey-man'd had thee," said their mother.

Jon and Emily looked at each other again. Jon handed the goose over to his mother.

"All of thee – upstairs!" said their mother to the children. "Jon's got to have a bath. There's hot water in the copper, Jon."

All the children left the mincepies and went through to the stairs. Emily followed them, and after her came Jon, on his way to get the tin bath from the yard. At the foot of the stairs he stopped her and whispered, "I think I know the answer . . . Is it 'A ghost'?"

Emily grinned, nodded, and went on up the stairs.

"If you want to hide something," Jon said, "put it in full view." And he went to fetch the bath.

Afterwards they had roast goose for Christmas dinner, and mincepies; and when Jon walked to work in the dark early the next morning, he didn't go across the fields, even though the twelve days of Christmas still had eleven days to run.

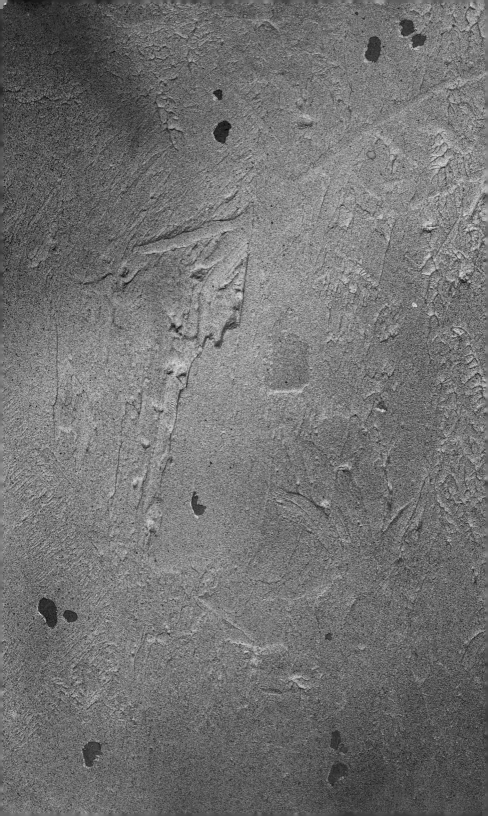